THE RED ZONE

NELSON HIGH RAIDERS #2

JORDAN FORD

BONUS GOODIES

If you're like me and you love to know how the author pictures the characters, then you're welcome to check out my Pinterest board for this series. Just click the link below:

https://www.pinterest.nz/melissapearlauthor/a-big-play-novels/

And if you'd like to sign up for my latest news, exclusive offers, plus receive a free introduction to the Ryder Bay series, then just **FOLLOW THIS LINK...**

https://www.subscribepage.com/JF_book_signup

———

www.jordanfordbooks.com

For Brody

The guy determined to walk his own journey. I love your strength and independence, and the fact you'll give anything a go. I can't wait to see what your future holds.

Love you, Broski.

1

ONE LOOK CAN CHANGE EVERYTHING

MACK

THE GYMNASIUM IS PACKED with color. As I look out across the student body my eyes are assaulted with a sea of orange and blue. Pompoms jiggle in the air to my left, and the stands in front are packed with expectation. Tomorrow is our final game, our chance to win the division championship title. It will be an epic way to end the season, and I want the entire school to be there, watching.

"Hey, Raiders!" I shout into the mic, pumping my fist in the air and feeling like a king.

The cheer is deafening, enhanced by the thundering of feet pounding on the bleachers. My team shouts and whoops behind me. Tyler even jumps up, using my shoulder as leverage, and pumps his fist in the air.

I grin and shove him off me before leaning back down to the mic. "It's been the best season this school has ever seen. Tomorrow, we're going to take away that title and go down as freaking Idaho legends!"

Laughter echoes through the cavernous space followed by another wave of cheering and applause.

I wait for it to simmer down before continuing. "We need you there tomorrow. So get your butts to Nelson stadium and be the loudest, most obnoxious crowd you've ever been. Make our day one to remember for the rest of our lives."

More thunder and cheering.

I raise my hands in the air and whoop. "Raiders!"

"Yeah!" Tyler shouts behind me, no doubt feeling as much like a celebrity as I do.

I can't deny that I kind of like it. Everyone in the stands loves me...us. We are gods in this place, and I don't want to think about the fact that in seven months, it'll all be over.

Enjoying the moment is my only priority today. Every time I think ahead, I'm sucked into a black vortex I don't want to face.

My smile is broad as I scan the crowd, taking in the enthusiasm, the smiling faces, the flirty looks from girls of all grades. I wink at a cute little freshman with dark brown curls. Her face flames with color and she dips her head. I laugh and step back from the podium so Coach Watson can rile the school up one last time before dismissing them to class.

"The big Mahoney, everybody!" Coach points at me while the students cheer…again.

I keep my smile in place, but don't miss the fact that Coach referred to me by my father's nickname. Yeah, I'm a legacy and I can tell ya, it's damn hard living up to the name of a dead man. Especially one as epic as my father.

I do my best.

I play. I party. I lead.

I live the life expected of me…the life my dad would want me to have. It's my attempt to fill the gaping wound left by his absence. Sometimes that hole feels small, and other times it's so big I don't think I can stand it.

But what more can I do?

"These guys have worked hard, trained hard, and they are the biggest threat in high school football in the state of Idaho. Heck, I'd be willing to challenge the whole nation with these guys. Don't you doubt that for a second!" Coach doesn't even need the mic; he has one of those booming voices. His voice vibrates throughout the gymnasium, creating yet another shockwave of support.

Tyler nudges me in the side, adjusting his letterman jacket as he checks out the cheer girls. Roxy glances over her shoulder, giving us both a sultry smile before waving her pompoms in the air.

Yeah, she's beautiful…and she knows it.

I shake my head and run my eyes down the line of players on the stage. Finn's jaw is clenched, his wide nostrils flaring slightly as he endures the pep rally. He hates these things. Although he plays center, he hates being front and center when it comes to a stage. I snicker, then grin when I catch Colt making eyes at his girl. The guy is so completely gone for Tori Lomax. I never thought any of us could fall that hard.

I follow his line of sight, looking for his cute little counterpart. I don't ever say it out loud, but I think she's kind of cool. She can talk football, and she's not all about how she looks. She's just a nice girl with a quirky sense of humor. I could never fall for someone like that, but I don't mind having her around.

I finally spot her in the stands. She's grinning at Colt, her large blue earring getting caught in her messy curls when she tips her head. She makes a funny face and sets about trying to untangle herself.

I snicker as she leans across to ask for help. Her best

friend leans in for the assist…and that's when I stop breathing for a second.

Because I see her—the most stunning creature I have ever laid eyes on.

Now, I'm not a romantic guy, okay? I can't stand chick flicks and I think those romantic novels my sister, Layla, reads are complete bullshit. But I swear I don't know what is coming over me right now.

I'm taken.

I'm stolen.

I'm owned.

I've never seen this girl before. She must be new, because if I ever had, I would have done something about it.

She's tall and lean, with waves of luscious hair and the kind of face you want to take in your hands and caress. Her eyes are… They're emeralds, and they're staring straight at me. My heart is pounding so hard I'm surprised the whole school can't hear it.

Her wide lips part, her eyes rounding for a quick moment. It's like she wants to look away from me but she can't.

I don't know what the hell's going on. I want time to

freeze. I want to stay locked in this…whatever the hell it is…for as long as possible.

What is wrong with me?

She blinks and jerks away from my intense stare, severing our connection. I can physically feel the loss and I'm totally confused.

Love at first sight does not exist.

I bite the inside of my cheek, studying her narrow, straight nose and the curve of her oval face.

The thought makes it hard to breathe, but I have to wonder if my aversion to romance is about to get kicked in the ass.

2

REALITY CHECK

KAIJA

HE WON'T STOP LOOKING at me.

Not that I really mind. He's completely gorgeous. My heart is beating so fast I actually feel sick. There's something in those dark brown eyes of his that is doing weird stuff to my body. I've had the hots for guys before, but this is something else. Something unfamiliar. And it's fully freaking me out.

The last thing I need to do is fall for the captain of the Nelson High football team.

Reality check, Kaija!

I'm in this country for less than three months. Ten weeks from now, I'll be on a plane, flying home to New

Zealand. I didn't come to Idaho to mess around with some super-hot McDreamy. I came here to…

I swallow and run slightly shaky fingers through my thick locks.

I came to experience something new.

My cheeks flush red at the lie. I can't think about the real reason I'm in America.

All I know is that falling for this school's celebrity would be the world's biggest mistake.

The intense attraction I'm feeling right now doesn't need an explanation. It needs to be ignored.

I force my gaze everywhere but the stage, trying to soak in the bizarre cacophony around me…but my traitorous eyes keep skimming the spot just to the right of the podium. I have no idea what the football coach is saying. My ears are ringing and my heart is still thumping like a bass drum—an incessant pounding that says, "Check out the hottie. Check out the hottie."

Snapping my eyes shut, I pull in a breath and crunch my teeth together.

This is ridiculous!

Love at first sight is for novels and romantic comedies. Whatever the hell I'm feeling right now must be pure lust or something. Maybe it's jet lag. I only arrived two nights ago; my body's still adjusting to the new time zone. The altitude in the plane made me loopy or something.

Surely, there's a logical explanation.

I fight the pull and force myself to look at Anderson. He's my host brother while I'm here. Our families have known each other for years and that's the only reason Mum let me come. A few months back, they invited me to experience a winter Christmas and to spend my New Zealand summer break checking out what life in the States is like. I've just finished Year 12, which is like my junior year of high school. Because of my sweet exam schedule, I finished about a week before everyone else. I flew out about seven hours after my final end-of-year exam. I wasn't going to do it at first. Who wants to give up their summer break to hang out in small-town Idaho? But then…

I clench my jaw, a nightmare image flashing through my brain.

The day before my exams began, I changed my mind. I couldn't get out of Auckland fast enough…and I'm already dreading my return.

Someone whistles behind me. I flinch at the sound while Anderson laughs at me.

"Totally ridiculous, right?" He nudges me with his

pointy elbow. "I hate these things. All this hype? It's such a crock."

I scan the ocean of orange and blue. The student body looks smaller than my school. Macleans College has around two thousand students from Year 9 - 13. I read that Nelson High was closer to the eight hundred mark. The amount of volume they are creating at this pep rally, though? The numbers could be argued. People don't cheer like this in New Zealand. We're more…low-key.

I snicker and look back at my blond friend. His hair is a muddy kind of color, like it couldn't decide whether to be brown or blond so settled for *br-ond*. He has one of those pointy kinds of faces with a sharp chin and a small mouth that curves into a tight, sardonic smile. To top it off, he has ice-blue eyes that are so keen I feel like they can see right through me. You wouldn't need to know anything about him to work out he's one of the smartest kids in the school.

He told me he's aiming for valedictorian.

I cast my eyes down our row, checking out his band of brainiac friends. So far they've all been really nice to me and I've tried to convince myself that this will be the best ten weeks I've ever had.

Another lie.

I'm going to give it my best shot, but I'm not stupid.

Anderson Foster and his Ivy League crew are not my usual peeps. I steal a quick look at the stage. The quarterback guy is grinning at one of his teammates, but his eyes soon travel back to me. I look down before he catches me checking him out.

I don't want it to be true, but guys like him... They are my people.

I won't go back, though. I can't become that girl again. So, Anderson and his mates it is.

Holding in my sigh, I lean over to hear what he's saying.

"...Thank God the season's nearly over," he shouts above the crowd.

The coach raises his fists and the student body jumps to their feet with a deafening roar.

"Now get your butts to class, and be great today!"

The students all cheer and I clap along with Anderson, who is now rolling his eyes. Nerves prickle my skin when I try to remember where my first class is. Anderson and his little sister, Dana, took me for a tour of the school yesterday, but it was a lot to take in. I'm guaranteed to get lost a few times over the next couple of weeks. Not that it really matters if I'm late to class. This trip is about the experience. None of my grades will count. Anderson's father has had heaps to do with the school over the years, so they're kind of doing him a favor by letting me attend.

It'll be a good experience.

At least that's what I'll keep telling myself.

I collect my bag and nestle it on my shoulder. A cute chick two rows down lets out a little squeal as this hot guy in a letterman jacket wraps his arm around her waist and swings her down off the step. She nestles her arm around his body and smiles up at him. The way he looks at her is so adorable. She says something that makes him laugh, then he kisses the side of her head and they walk out of the gymnasium together. I notice a few cheerleaders glaring after them. One of the tall blondes and a girl with long dark hair scowl. I can already tell what those catty girls are thinking.

Whoever snagged one of "their" players doesn't belong. I guess schools the world over are the same. There are always social boundaries, and when someone tries to cross them, trouble ensues. A shudder runs down my spine, memories haunting me as I study the cute couple in front of us.

"That's Colt Burgess and Tori Lomax. Them getting together has been the big scandal this semester." Anderson rolls his eyes. He does that a lot.

"I take it the football guys rule this school."

"Jocks and cheerleaders." He pokes out his tongue like he's going to be sick.

I grin. "How very high school movie of them."

He laughs and holds out his hand to help me off the last bleacher. I'm quite capable of jumping down on my own, but I don't want to be rude. With a tight smile, I take his hand. The way he smiles at me is just a little too hopeful, so I wriggle out of his grasp as soon as I'm standing on the shiny floor.

"Yeah, the social lines in this school are marked in permanent ink. I'm telling you now, you want to stick with your own kind. Tori and Colt have caught some major flack from the cheerleaders over their relationship, but the guy seems really protective of her, so it's working for now."

"They make a cute couple," the short girl beside me pipes up. "I hope they last forever." Her smile is dreamy as she stares after them.

"Ugh, Shelby, please do not start referring to them as *Cori* or *Tolt*. I will have to disassociate myself from you if you do." She giggles while he grimaces. "You're so romantic."

"What's wrong with a little romance?" Her deep dimples are accentuated when she smiles like that. "I wouldn't mind one of the Raiders sweeping me off my feet. Tori Lomax is the luckiest girl in this school…and that status will not change until Mack Mahoney scores himself a girl." The way she wistfully sighs Mack's name makes it obvious how much she wants it to be her.

"Mack doesn't need to score himself anything. The girls in this school practically kiss the ground he walks on." Anderson's derisive tone is impossible to miss, as is Shelby's blush.

I don't really know who they're talking about.

The guy next to Anderson leans into the conversation. "The guy's the quarterback and captain; technically, he should be dating Roxanne Carmichael. She's the head cheerleader."

My nose wrinkles. "Isn't that a bit cliché?"

"High school movie, remember? Welcome to Hollywood." Anderson chuckles as we walk through the double doors.

I'm desperately trying to ignore the way my heart took off when I worked out that Mack is the guy who caught me with his intense brown gaze...or maybe it was the broad set of his shoulders and the way he carries himself with such confidence. Or it could be the way his face looks like it's been chiseled out of marble and sanded to perfection. Or maybe it's his height.

Nope. It's the eyes. Those chocolate brown goodies.

Gripping my bag strap, I follow my host brother to the right, refusing to glance over my shoulder to check to see where Mack is. I can almost feel his gaze on me, and like hell I'm giving myself away.

Hunching my shoulders, I pick up my pace and start praying he's not in any of my classes today.

Anderson was spot-on with his whole quarterback-dates-cheerleader theory.

We may not have cheerleaders at my school, and we definitely don't have football. But we do have a super-hot rugby team and they go for the netball girls. I swallow down the bile lurching up my throat, trying to forget the fact that I used to be one of those girls, flaunting my perfect high ponytail and ultra-short netball uniform, with enough attitude to sink the *Titanic*.

3

THE LOWDOWN

MACK

AS PER USUAL, the cafeteria is crammed with human traffic, tasteless food, and the ever-present buzz of anticipation. What's gonna go down today? Will there be any drama?

I'm usually immune to most of that crap. Our table is a little insular, I'll admit. People tend to watch us, not the other way around. But today…I'm like a freaking hawk. My eyes rove the noisy space until I find what I'm looking for. She's tall, she's lean, and her face makes my heart kick out of rhythm. I scratch the back of my short hair with a frown, wondering why the hell I'm torturing myself. I should be turning the opposite direction and checking out the cheerleaders at my table. Roxy's been eyeing me up for weeks. We've been doing the casual flirting thing, making out at a few parties. I'm not after anything more than a good time though…and I have to admit, she's pretty sexy entertainment. We're really good at getting our flirt on when we're around each other, and she knows I don't do serious. I've always been very open about that.

But that emerald-eyed beauty? She's doing weird shit to my brain, and *serious* suddenly sounds enticing, which is so screwed up because I don't even know her name!

Unfortunately, I don't think I'll be able to let it go until I do something about it.

She's sitting with Anderson Foster right now. I could provide today's drama by heading over there and introducing myself, but I don't really want the entire school watching when I make my first move.

I glance at my buddies around me. Tyler is playing wink and smirk with Michelle. She's sitting in between Roxy and my sister, Layla. He's never told me so, but I think he's actually got the hots for Roxy. I'm pretty sure he hasn't done anything about it because of me. He also knows not to go anywhere near my sister, so Michelle is the play of the day. I wonder which cheer girl it will be tomorrow.

Colt and Finn are laughing about something. My eyes glide past them and I notice Tori stand up from the new girl's table. She's so short I didn't see her behind the towering Foster. She says something that makes her face light with a smile before patting her friend Amy on the shoulder and waving goodbye to everyone. With her patchwork satchel over one shoulder—no doubt homemade—and a colorful scarf over the other, she leaves her friends and heads our way.

Large, nutmeg curls bounce around her face as she does this little skip thing and stops by our table.

"Hey." She grins, resting her arm on Colt's shoulder.

"Hey, baby." Colt smiles up at her and she leans down to give him a quick kiss.

I catch Tyler's grimace out of the corner of my eye. He still doesn't get why one of the most eligible guys in this school has settled for a girl who's not part of our crowd.

He'll figure it out eventually.

I raise my eyebrows with a smile. "'Sup, Pixie Girl?"

"Nothin' much. Just swinging by for a little candy before I have to go to class."

Colt's face lights with an even bigger grin, if that's actually possible, and he wraps his arm around her waist, yanking her closer.

"So, uh, who's the new chick?" I start talking before they can start making out like nobody else exists.

Tori tucks a curl behind her ear and glances over her shoulder.

"The one with Anderson Foster and all the geek club kids," I help her out.

Tori spins back with a dry glare. "You know they're not called geek clubs, right? They have actual names, like debate team and student council."

"Wiseass academy, brainiac brigade," Tyler mumbles.

"People you'll be working for one day." Tori winks and Tyler has to give in with a snicker. He scratches between his eyebrows with his middle finger and Tori tips her head back with a laugh.

Colt sends our friend a silent warning to quit while he's ahead. When it comes to Tori, he won't tolerate any bullshit. The guy's more protective of her than I am of Layla.

"Do you know anything about her?" I lift my chin toward the *honor roll* table, hoping I look casually curious and not desperate to know.

"Oh, um, yeah, she's an exchange student from New Zealand."

"Where is that again?" Tyler asks.

"It's near Australia," Colt murmurs. "Rugby, right? They do that warrior dance thing before their games."

Tori shrugs. "I don't know, but *The Lord of the Rings* was filmed there, which is way cool…and not at all geeky." She points at Tyler before he can say anything.

He just smirks at her. "You're good, Pixie Girl. Those elf chicks are hot."

Tori's face scrunches with distaste while Finn looks behind him as he tries to spot the new girl.

"What's her name?" I twirl my empty water bottle on the table, forcing myself not to follow Finn's line of sight.

"Oh, it's kind of unusual." Tori's nose wrinkles. "Ky-ya. Just think hi-ya with a K."

"Ky-ya." I test it out with a grin, then notice Colt and Tori smirking at me. I jolt back in my seat and scowl at them. "What?"

Tori grins. "She is gorgeous."

I flash her a pleading look that I hope everyone else will miss, then settle on an expression that hopefully says, *I don't care.*

Tori's grey eyes sparkle, but she pulls her mouth into line, dipping her head before drip-feeding me a little more info. "She arrived like a day ago, I think, and she's staying with the Fosters. And that's pretty much all I know." Her lips purse to the side as she eyes me up again. My nonchalance is fading as my mind starts ticking over with excuses to stop by the Fosters' place. They live next door to Roxy Carmichael. Maybe I could somehow…

"She has this really adorable accent, and seems super nice. Maybe you should try talking to her." Tori's playful expression makes me fold, and I decide the only way to play this and not come off looking like a total idiot is to claim the shit out of it.

Puffing out my chest, I rise to my full height and give the guys my best smirk. "Believe me, I intend to."

Colt slaps the table with a laugh. "I've seen that look before. Watch out, new girl."

Tori wriggles her eyebrows with a giggle, but the sound is cut short when Layla and Roxy get up from the table and walk behind me. Pixie Girl dips her head and focuses on the top of Colt's head as they pass.

Our star playmaker glares at the girls and their demeaning smirks. I'm kind of embarrassed that one of them's my sister, but I can't exactly tell her who she can and can't like. It's a hard enough job monitoring the *guys* she has in her life—I don't have time to worry about the girls.

I think Tori's cool, but she's her own island and when it

comes to this school, bridges between countries and islands are not built in a hurry.

Tori places her hand on Colt's cheek and turns him away, gazing down at him with a sweet smile and shaking her head.

"It doesn't matter," she whispers, then presses her lips to his.

The bell rings, a shrill sound that slices through the awkward tension. Colt stands tall, sliding his arm down Tori's back and holding her close.

"I'll walk you to class," he murmurs before kissing her curls. "Catch you guys later."

They wave goodbye and walk out the other exit. It's a longer way around, but it saves them having to cross paths with the cheerleaders again. I kind of hate that it's like that. I don't like any kind of division in the team, especially before the final, but thankfully most of the guys couldn't care who Colt dates. And as long as the cheerleaders keep their claws retracted, we should be good.

I slowly collect my bag and drag it up to my shoulder. Ky-ya is walking next to Anderson, listening to him prattle on about something. I can't hear what he's saying, but I can tell by the look on his face that he's trying to impress her. Okay, so the guy's not blind... and neither am I.

Looks like I've got myself some competition. I internally snicker. *Yeah, right!*

I study the pair as they head for the exit, not feeling threatened. She looks kind of bored, if you ask me, but then the king of geekdom says something that makes her smile.

The shape of her mouth when she grins is so beautiful —the point of her chin and those straight white teeth.

She looks down as she walks past me, and I can't help wondering if she's intentionally trying to avoid eye contact. It only confirms my notion that something happened between us in the gym this morning.

And it only makes me more determined to do something about it.

4

THE STARES

KAIJA

THE TEACHER'S accent makes me smile. He's talking about the US government and I'm totally lost. I know there's a president and stuff, but this country is run very different than little ol' New Zealand. That's why I wanted to take this class, to learn something totally new. Truth is, though, I'm finding it really hard to focus.

It doesn't help that every time I look up from my note-taking at least two sets of eyes are glancing—or just outright staring—at me. I smile at a few of them, but it's getting old pretty fast.

I get it. I'm the new girl with the weird accent. I come from some exotic little country that doesn't always make it onto world maps—although that's drastically improving thanks to Peter Jackson and his epic fantasy movies.

A few months ago, it wouldn't have bothered me. I'm used to being checked out. Hell, if I'm honest, I used to love it. Not to be arrogant, but I'm kind of easy on the eyes—I'm tall, slender, decent chest, nice complexion, good bone structure. I don't know why, but guys seem to like that combo. And believe me, I used to wear clothes and makeup that would accentuate every one of those features.

The thing is, though, all those gazes of lust or admiration that I'd grown accustomed to? Yeah, they changed. Eyes that used to love me started staring at me with looks of horror and disdain, curiosity and scandal. I guess I deserved it, after what I did, but…

I couldn't take it.

And so I fled.

Now I'm halfway around the world and I'm still trying to dodge those stares.

Grinding my teeth together, I grip the pen in my fingers and focus back on the teacher and his American accent.

"So, who can tell me why this amendment to the Constitution was so hotly debated? What made it so controversial at the time?"

I glance around the room and see a few hands tentatively rise. Some kid who looks like he could be Anderson's intellectual clone starts droning on about some policy I've never heard of. My brain immediately starts to wander…to that hot-looking quarterback.

Far out, those eyes. That body. The proud little smirk on his face when he was telling everyone they were going to win the division championship. He thinks he's such hot shit. I'll go to the grave before admitting how sexy his cocky arrogance is.

I wish I wasn't attracted to guys like that. They're no good for me.

I speak from experience, and I will not be going down that path again.

Sensing a new set of eyes on me, I shift my head and meet Roxanne Carmichael's icy gaze. I turn away with an eye roll. Crap. I was really hoping we wouldn't be in any of the same classes.

She flounced over to the Fosters' house yesterday, to introduce herself and to welcome the new girl. I knew exactly what she was doing. Keep your enemies close, right? Popular girls in New Zealand are just the same. Pretty, mysterious new girls are a potential threat to their status. The best way to deal with it is to either bring them into your circle so you can control them or ice them out and make them public enemy number one.

Much to her aggravation—and no doubt mine—I refused to swoon and giggle. I don't want to be pulled into that social circle again. So, I politely declined and painted a big, red target on my forehead.

I don't care.

I'm not here to be popular and make friends.

In fact, I'm striving for the opposite.

A brutal memory that has the power to cripple me flashes through my brain and I'm reminded once again why I'm taking the path of most resistance. It'd be so easy to walk into Roxy's world. I'd be comfortable there.

But…

My nostrils flare as my eyes start to sting.

I won't go back.

I can't become that bitchy girl again.

5

MACK-ATTACK

MACK

THE DAY IS FINALLY OVER. This would usually make me feel pretty good, but not today, because I still haven't spoken to my green-eyed beauty. I scan the hallways for her as I leave calculus, wondering where her locker might be. Probably next to Anderson Foster's. My lip curls as I hike my bag higher onto my shoulder.

Tyler lifts his chin at me as I glide past. He's probably wondering why I didn't stop to flirt with the posse of cheerleaders giggling at one of his jokes. I'm not in the mood. I've got more important things to do.

Now, where the hell is Ky-ya's locker?

I turn the corner to subtly check out the hallway opposite my physics class when I catch sight of Samantha Carmichael. Skater girl might give me the goods. She lives right next door to the stunning exchange student.

"Hey, Sammy." I make a clicking noise to get her attention.

She stops short and spins to give me a droll glare. Her long straight hair wafts around her face as she approaches me, her beloved skateboard tucked against her hip. She's a bit of an enigma, this one. She's got this mysterious quality about her, with one of those refined, angular faces. She looks like a warrior elf, and I can picture her kicking serious ass. I'm pretty sure she scares the shit out of most girls, but all the guys like her because she's….well, she's practically one of us.

The junior stops in front of me and crosses her arms. "I'm not a horse, Mack-Attack. You don't have to go clicking at me."

I grin. "I was just wondering if you could help me out."

"Oh, really?" Her keen blue eyes strip me bare while a smirk tugs at her wide mouth.

I roll my eyes, then check the crowd shifting past us before asking, "I was just wondering if you've met the new kid yet."

"You mean the incredibly hot girl who's moved in next door? Yeah, she's really not my type."

My mouth pops opens before I can stop it. I didn't know Sammy swung that way. I mean, I'm not entirely surprised—

Her face hardens and her fist shoots into my arm before I even see it coming.

"Oof!"

"I'm not into girls, you douchebag. I mean she's not a skater chick."

"Got it." I rub my arm while fighting a chuckle.

Her dry glare helps douse my humor. I'm trying to get the goods and I won't get shit if Sammy decides she doesn't want to play. She starts to angle away from me so I blurt out, "Sorry. I just…" I clear my throat, scratching the back of my neck and trying not to smile. "What about Roxy?"

Sammy's head tips to the side, her long straight locks falling over her shoulder. "Yeah, it's funny. I thought they'd hit it off, but Kiwi Girl's given our little Roxette the brush off."

"Kiwi?"

"It means a New Zealander. Get with the lingo, dude."

I grin, then rub my mouth, loving the nickname—Kiwi Girl.

"I guess it goes to show that extreme beauty doesn't automatically make someone a bitch. I kinda like that." She shrugs, obviously thinking about her sister. They are complete opposites in every way (except their eye color)…and I'm pretty sure they hate each other. It's kind of sad, but I get it. I can't stand my stepbrother. Yeah, we're not blood, but we're still supposed to act like family and that's damn difficult when the guy you're meant to call *brother* is a complete asshole.

"Catch you later, Romeo. Good luck wooing the newbie. If you ask me, she's going to be a tough nut to crack. You sure you got the balls to handle it?"

I grab my crotch and give her my best smirk. She sees right through it and starts laughing, shaking her head as she drops her board to the ground.

"Her locker's down the next hallway. May the force be with you."

She jumps on her board and kicks off, weaving around the students like a pro. She makes it all the way to the end of the hall before being yelled at by a teacher.

"Miss Carmichael!"

You hear that a lot in this place.

A pair of girls with flirty smiles passes me. I grin at them, listening to their tittering as I saunter away. It's a nice confidence booster. I turn the corner in search of the only girl who's ever sparked something stronger than mild interest. It's bizarre, considering I haven't even spoken to her yet. I must be all kinds of crazy.

I spot her halfway down the hall, her face scrunched with concentration as she gazes into her locker. My heart starts buzzing, sending volts of heady pleasure zipping down to my toes. This is insane!

Puffing out my chest, I swagger over with the smile that makes most girls give me their dreamy eyes.

"Hey." I stop beside her, gliding my hand into my pocket and trying to figure out why the hell I suddenly feel so nervous.

She glances up at me, her green eyes like a drug. I stare into them, transfixed. They round for a second before her head snaps back to her locker.

"Hello." Her voice is soft and clipped.

I'm close enough to get a whiff of her shampoo. I glance down at her shiny locks—they have blonde streaks running through the dark cinnamon brown. I have to resist the urge to reach out and run my fingers through the fruity tendrils. They smell so damn good.

A tendon in her neck strains, her nostrils flaring slightly as she takes in a sharp breath.

"Can I help with something?" I get a full taste of her *kiwi* accent and instantly love it.

A slow smile draws my lips north and I lean against the metal locker beside hers. "I just wanted to say hi and welcome you to the school."

"Someone's already done that." Her sharp tone throws me off. Most girls would be turning to face me by now, maybe blushing a little or doing that cute little laugh they do when they're getting their flirt on.

Ky-ya's giving me a solid stonewalling. I glance down at the binder in her arms and notice the way her name is spelled at the top—Kaija Bennett.

My forehead crinkles. "I'm Mack."

"Yeah, I heard. Star quarterback, captain of the football team." She slams her locker shut, gripping the binder to her chest and looking straight at me. "Seriously hot shit."

Her slightly mocking tone and the glint in her eyes makes me stand straight. I put on my best smolder and lean a little closer. If I take one more step forward, her mouth will be pressed against my chin. She doesn't seem flustered by my move; if anything, she knows exactly what I'm trying to do. Her gaze travels down my body with a look of contempt.

I don't understand what's happening right now. This usually works.

But she's obviously no ordinary girl—yet another thing to like about her.

A bemused smile curls my lips as I decide to play her little game. "I don't know what it's like down in kiwi-land, but in this country, when someone introduces themselves, the polite thing to do is shake their hand and tell them your name."

Her lips twitch with a grin, her right eyebrow peaking as she drills me with those keen eyes. "I'm guessing that you already know my name, oh great captain. I can tell that you expect me to bat my eyelashes, maybe giggle a little bit and be desperately waiting for you to ask me out. I'll save you some trouble, shall I?" She flicks her dark hair over her shoulder and gives me her cheesiest smile. "My name's Kaija, and I'm not interested in dating someone who thinks the sun shines out his ass."

I blink slowly, because that's all I can really do at this point. I have never been spoken to like this before in my life. People love me. Chicks want to be with me—I have a phone directory worth of names and numbers I could dial anytime.

Yet I'm compelled to keep standing here staring at this sassy-mouthed beauty.

What the *hell* is wrong with me?

She gives me another stunning smile that makes it hard to breathe.

"Good luck at the game tomorrow, superstar. Go the mighty Raiders. I hope you get that victory, because you're not scoring anything here." She points to herself with a little smirk, then glides past me like I'm nothing more than a speck of dust.

"I…" I turn to watch her leave, still trying to wrap my brain around what just went down. A snickering to my right catches my attention and I look over my shoulder to see two of Anderson's nerdy friends laughing at me. I scan the hall and notice that everyone within a five-foot radius was eavesdropping on the exchange and they're all giving me open-mouthed stares or giggling behind their hands.

This has got to be the most abnormal day of my life.

I stare down the hall again, watching Kaija disappear around the corner. Most guys would take their leave now, accept defeat with a little dignity, and move on to better pastures, so to speak.

But I'm not most guys, and that little chat I just endured hasn't done anything to put me off. If I'm honest, her feisty little eyes as she put me in my place were nothing but a red-hot turn-on. If she thinks I'm going to back away, she's got another thing coming.

She may not think I'm hot shit right now, but she will. I saw the way she looked at me in the gym this morning, and I'm not ready to believe that something didn't pass between us.

6

NEW GAME—NEW RULES

KAIJA

MY HEART WAS GOING for it when I walked away from Mack and his sexy little smirk yesterday. How I didn't give in to that cocky charm, I'll never know. I acted like a world-class bitch, which is why my heart is once again racing. Because he's standing on that field in his football uniform, commanding an army of players. He's in full control and it's a total turn-on. This is bad. I mean, this is really bad.

My last boyfriend could lead a crowd, but not like this.

Mack's players protect him like he's their king. I know that's got something to do with the actual game and his position, but still. There's a reverence there, and I can't help admiring it.

Dammit!

I cannot let a guy like him under my skin.

That's why I was so rude to him. I wanted to put him off as quickly as I could. But the way his face lit up when he saw me sitting in the stands today totally gave away the fact that my ice queen routine has only ignited him.

He's used to getting what he wants. But I'm here to play things differently, not fall back into old traps.

Guys like that are bad for me.

I know this.

So, why am I feeling this way?

Why does Mack have to be so…? Well, he's not perfect, but he's *soooooo* my type.

I should just go, but I don't really know where I am in Nelson and finding my way back to the Fosters' house seems too hard to handle, even with the GPS on my phone. From the look on Dana's face, I doubt I can talk her into leaving. And Anderson is doing some intense study thing at the library today, so I don't really want to disturb him.

Glancing at my watch, I realize I've only been here for thirty minutes. This is going to be the longest day of my life. From the little I do know of football, the games are really long because they stop the clock all the time. Squirming in my freezing-cold seat, I tuck my gloved hands under my thighs and force a smile at my host sister. Dana Foster is in the ninth grade and wants to be cool more than anything. The problem is, she tries too hard. When we first arrived, she practically skipped over to the cheer squad to say hi. They all looked at her like she was a piece of chewed-up gum. A couple smiled politely before turning their backs. She seemed unfazed, because she then went on to wave and scream at the Raiders team when they ran out of the tunnel. That's how Mack spotted me.

So, Dana has a lot to learn. I could teach her everything she needs to know, but I'm not going to. I don't want her becoming what I was.

I turn my gaze back to the field and try to figure out what's really going on. Dana is too busy swooning and drooling to give me any kind of rundown. Rather than telling me about the actual rules of football, she spends the whole time going, "See number 28? So freaking hot. His name's Tyler Schumann, and he's around at the Carmichaels' quite a bit because he's friends with Sammy. I think he's got the hots for Roxanne and is using Sammy as an excuse to spend time there."

I nod, going for unimpressed. It's not that hard. From the glimpses I've caught of Tyler, he's a raving sex fiend who's after Roxy for only one thing. I curl my lip and turn away from his blue and orange helmet.

A flustered girl with wild curls plunks down next to me. "Oh my gosh, I am so late! I'm never late." She looks at me and keeps talking like we're friends or something. "My mom's car, which is like a hundred years old, broke down and I had to run." She tugs on her orange scarf. "So, what have I missed?" Her eyes dart to the scoreboard and then back to the field, her face lighting with a smile.

That's right. She's the girl who was sitting near me in the cafeteria yesterday. I can't remember her name.

"Oh, and number 27." Dana nudges me. "He's like the playmaker and super sexy."

"And my boyfriend," the girl beside me mumbles.

Dana suddenly notices her and lets out a choking gasp before ducking behind my shoulder.

I glance at the new girl beside me and she winks. Her smile is broad and sparkling as she sticks out her hand. "I'm Tori."

"Hi, I'm Kaija." I shake her hand and smile.

"Yeah, I know. Amy was telling me about you. Exchange student, right? We kind of sat near each other in the cafeteria yesterday."

"I remember. Amy… She's Anderson's study partner, right?"

"Or his biggest competition." Tori giggles. "I think the only reason they study together is to keep an eye on what the other's doing. They're both vying for valedictorian." Tori shakes her head with a grin. "She's my bestie, but she's not here today because she's really not a football fan, plus she works all the time. She's saving for Harvard. She's not sure if she'll get a scholarship or not, and she's freaking out a little bit. I mean, her parents can probably afford it, but they're all about earning your own way and stuff. There's no way they're going to let her miss out on Harvard, though."

Tori talks so fast it's almost hard to keep up. A wide smile spreads across my face as I listen to her. She's watching the field the whole time she's talking, tensing and moving with the ball as each play is made.

"Crap," she mutters.

I follow her frown and see Mack running off the field, slapping hands with the new guys coming on.

"Why are they changing?" I didn't mean to say it out loud. I know I'm a newbie, but I don't want to come across like a complete ignorant.

"Oh, the defensive team. So, the Bears. Grrr, the Bears. We hate the Bears." The venom in her voice tells me there's more to that story. "They just got a turnover, so now our defensive team is running on to make sure they stay away from our end zone."

I watch her pointing finger and figure the end zone is kind of like the try line in rugby.

"So, what team is your boyfriend on?"

"He's a running back, so he's part of the offensive team. They're on the field for all the attacking plays and then defense comes out for…well, you know, defensive plays."

"Okay." I nod, enjoying her explanation. I don't want to disrupt the game for her too much, but I'm finding it kind of interesting. Coming from a sports-obsessed family, I'm keen to know more. "So, when you say *play*, is that like one set of the 'hut, hut' thing?"

Tori giggles and nods at me. "Pretty much. They set each time, then the ball gets snapped to the quarterback, and then play begins. The whole point is to try and make a down, which is 10 yards. So you get four chances to make a down. If you do, you get another four, and if you don't, the ball gets turned over to the other team."

"Oh, so a little like rugby league, then. In that you get six tackles to score a try and if you don't make it then the ball gets turned over."

Tori nods, but it's obvious that she has no idea what I'm talking about.

"You've heard of rugby, right?"

"Colt has. He says you guys do a warrior dance before the games or something."

I grin. "The *haka*. Yeah, I guess it is kind of like a warrior dance, but it's more of a challenge. Our native race, the Maoris, used to do these challenges before battles to try and scare off the enemy." I can't help snickering at Tori's wide-eyed expression. They must think I come from the weirdest country in the world. I shrug. "I like it."

"Believe me, so does my boyfriend. He showed me a YouTube clip last night. He thinks it's way fierce."

I grin, appreciating her attempt to make me feel just a little less alien.

I turn back to the game, suddenly grateful she sat down next to me. There's something about Tori that's so open and sweet. She reminds me a little of Eloise—a girl I used to play with in primary school. We were best friends.

A deep sadness seeps into me as I quietly grieve. If only she hadn't had to leave, maybe I would have turned out more like Tori. I wouldn't have been caught up with the wrong crowd and turned into the world's worst human being. And I wouldn't have ended up hurting sweet little Eloise when she came back to New Zealand.

Clenching my jaw, I focus back on the game, my eyes honing in on number 31—the quarterback. I wish I'd stop doing that. I don't want to watch him. I don't want to like the way his defined muscles move—the pull of his thigh as he pivots back, the strain of his arm as he throws a beautiful spiral down the field. Number 28 races down the line, covered by a bunch of guys in blue and orange. They crunch into the red and black players, downing their foes so Tyler can catch the ball and jump across the line. He drops the ball down in the end zone while a raucous cheer erupts around me. Tori is on her feet already, screaming like a banshee.

Dana jumps up on the other side. "Woohoo! Go Raiders!"

The cheerleaders are going crazy, their pompoms dancing while they kick their feet in the air and jump up and down. This is insane.

I kind of like it.

Getting to my feet, I clap along with the frenzied fans, laughing as a few guys careen into Tyler, slapping his helmet and jumping onto his back.

Number 27 looks up into the stands. For a second, I think he's staring at me, but then I hear a kissing noise beside me and notice Tori blowing them his way.

"She's so lucky." Dana simmers beside me.

I give her a strange look but don't have time to analyze it, because the field is already reset and play is about to resume. Taking a seat beside Tori, I lean in as she starts explaining different types of plays to me, and how they all have these funny names. I get absorbed in the lesson, enjoying the game more and more as the time ticks by.

7

IT'S TIME TO PLAY

MACK

THIS GAME IS GOING to kill me. I hate playing the Bears. Their code of conduct is seriously flawed. They play dirty and seem to get off on it. I know they're out to prove themselves and win the division title this year, but like hell we're going to give it to them.

I round up my offense, pulling them into the huddle before setting up for the play. Will is out with a bleeding face thanks to a brutal tackle from my asshole stepbrother. It took everything in me not to go after him, but my mother nearly disowned me last time I did that. She thinks the sun shines out Derek's butt because he's the son of her precious sweetheart, Martin.

Glancing into the stands, I spot her in the third row,

her fingers clasped together as she endures the last twenty seconds of play. Martin is beside her, looking just as edgy. They want both teams to win, but that's not the way it works. There can only be one victor, and it's going to be the Nelson High Raiders.

We're three points down with only 20 seconds left on the clock. We have to win this thing. A sweet little touchdown ought to do it. Then we'll be division champions for the second year running.

I can't help thinking of my dad as we form an offensive huddle. Coach wants me to play it safe and run the ball. It's a good move, and Colt's probably fast enough to pull it off. But defense has been on him the entire game and with only twenty seconds of play, I don't know if we can make the forty yards we need.

Resting my hands on my knees, I clench my jaw, then make a snap decision. "Okay, guys, we're running a flea flicker."

Tyler hisses. "Risky play, dude. Did coach really call that?"

I give him a hard glare. "Don't chicken out on me now, man. I need you to catch the damn ball. We're not losing to these assholes." I turn to Colt. "You take first handoff, then pass it back to me. They're going to be on you like white on rice, but wait until the last second before flicking it back to me. Ty, I'll be looking for you in the left corner."

"You got it." Colt and Tyler both nod. Although Tyler questioned my call, he never fights me once the decision's been made. The calm determination in his gaze is all the confidence I need. We can do this.

"Finn, your boys set?"

"We've got your back, Mack-Attack." He grins.

"Let's win this title!" I shout, then clap my hands. "Break!"

We jog into position. Derek's sneering gaze is on me. Man, I hate that guy.

"Alright, set!" I call down the line. "Green 16! Green 16! Hut! Hut!"

Finn snaps the ball. It powers into my hands and I grip the skin and spin, passing it off to Colt who is, as always, running the perfect line. As predicted, the Bears' defense charges after him. Jogging back, I position myself for the pass. It pops into the air and I jump to catch it, landing on solid feet before angling my body and throwing back my arm. The ball fires out of my hand and flies towards the left corner of the field. Tyler is already running for it, his arms extended for the catch. My heart's stuck in my throat as I watch the ball arc and descend…straight into Tyler's hands.

"Yes!" I roar, running after the wide receiver as he fends off one player and springs over another. His body spins in the air and he crunches into the end zone. "Yeah!" I'm jumping like a maniac, laughing and cheering as Colt grabs my shirt and bolts down the field with me.

We pile on top of Tyler like he's just won a gold medal. I can't believe we pulled it off.

But then I can.

'Cause we're the Nelson High Raiders.

The cheers are near deafening as we untangle ourselves and stand to survey the crowd. A goofy grin pulls my cheeks so wide my face starts to hurt. Raising my arms in the air, I release a loud whoop and the crowd erupts all over again. In true Tyler style, he jumps on my back with a loud "Yee-hah!"

"Yes!" Colt slams into me from the other side, slapping my helmet and laughing.

Finn wraps his mammoth arms around us all and we jump in a circle like some tween girls at a One Direction concert. We're too hyped to think about the fact that we probably look like a bunch of knuckle-nuts.

The Bears stalk off the field, throwing us evil glares that I'm only just aware of. They can look at us however the hell they want. I'm tempted to turn to

Derek and give him the finger but our parents are watching, not to mention a row of eager scouts. I don't want to come across like a complete douche. I flip him off in my head when he shouts some insult over his shoulder. As soon as the f-bomb leaves his lips, I tune out and turn my back on him.

Colt whips off his helmet. He's freaking shining right now. The Boise State coaches told him if he played well today, there'd be a verbal offer coming his way. I muss his hair then wrap my arm around his neck. "We're gonna be Broncos, man!"

He whoops to try and hide his emotion, but I'm pretty sure the second he gets alone or with his girl, he's gonna start blubbering like a baby. His dreams are finally coming true.

Our future's set.

Too bad that thought feels more like a gunshot wound than an excuse to party.

I will the thought away and look into the stands. Mom's cheering and smiling at me. Martin wraps his arm around her shoulders and says something to make her laugh. She gazes up at him and they start kissing. I roll my eyes and look to the other stands where I last saw Kaija. She's standing between Tori and Dana Foster, laughing down at the girls jumping on either side of her.

Whipping off my helmet, I shake the coaches' hands and nod at their congratulations. "Thank you, Coach... Thank you... Thanks." I don't really hear what they're saying to me. The crowd is still going for it, and I'm too buzzed from the win to absorb anything more than smiling faces right now.

My cheeks heat with color when Coach Watson reaches me. He shakes his head and mutters, "Just like your father, kid. You're gonna go far."

"Thank you, Coach." I swallow, then step aside so he can keep congratulating the team. I turn to watch him, my chest swelling with Papa Bear pride. I've been working with these guys for years now and we've all come so far. This win has been epic...and Kaija saw the whole thing.

I spin to seek her out again. She's collecting her things and chatting with Tori as if they're long-time friends. I nudge Colt's elbow and point to the stands as Tori fights the departing crowd and heads for the front row. Dana's doing the same and Kaija is forced to follow them.

Yes!

The coaches and local news reporters are waiting for team photos, but I'm sure they can spare a minute. I follow Colt as he grins and heads to the sidelines, stopping by the concrete wall to chat with Tori. "Hey, baby. You enjoy that?" he calls up to her.

"Once I got my heart out of my throat." She laughs, then stretches down to touch his hand.

He jumps up and kisses her fingers.

Kaija's hovering behind her, trying not to look at me. I approach the fence with a confident smile. "Hey, Kiwi Girl. What'd you think of the game?"

Her narrow nostrils flare slightly. She flicks her hair over her shoulder and crosses her arms. "It was okay, I guess."

"Aw, come on, you can do better than that." I wink. "I saw you watching. You liked it."

"Maybe." Her full lips fight a smile. "But certainly not because of you."

Colt goes still beside me, frowning up at the new girl while Dana's mouth opens in horror. Tori bites her lips together and looks at the ground.

I smirk. "You don't like seeing men pushing it to the max on a field? I thought you'd be into that kind of thing. You know, with your rugby warriors and all that." I don't mean to sound quite so condescending.

Kaija's eyes light with a playful sparkle as her lips purse to the side. She's fighting a grin, I can tell. Clearing her throat, she manages to regain control of her expression and gazes down at me with her own little smirk. "Unlike you, our rugby *warriors* don't prance around a field in padding, helmets, and ballerina tights. We breed them tough in little ol' New Zealand. You know, real men, playing real sports."

Her dark eyebrows rise while my lips part in slight wonder at her insult. She looks like she's fighting a laugh—like she can't believe she just said that. Her gaze shifts away from mine, hitting the fence to our right before diving down to the concrete at her feet.

I glance at Colt, who is now glaring at her. Tori lets out a nervous, high-pitched titter. Slapping her hand over her mouth, she looks at Colt and gives him a silent apology. He shakes his head and winks at her then throws me a *what the hell* kind of look before starting to snicker himself.

"See you around, tough guy." Kaija spins on her heel, dashing away like she's running from a tornado.

All I can do is stand there and stare at the way her hips sway from side to side as she ascends the concrete steps. Dana scrambles after her while I gaze at Kiwi Girl's backside, a slow smile spreading on my lips.

"Feisty," I murmur.

"I was thinking bitchy, but okay," Colt mutters.

My smile grows even wider as I glance between the sweet couple in front me and compare their gag-worthy interactions to mine and Kaija's.

"She's only bitchy 'cause of me." I start to laugh. Maybe it's the high of winning, or the exhaustion of playing the toughest game I ever have, but I can't help feeling like those insults were said in jest, and the main purpose was to try to put me off.

It's not going to work.

She wants me...just like I want her. But, hey, if she likes to flirt dirty then so be it. I can flirt dirty too.

This challenge just got that much more enticing.

8

AND SO IT BEGINS

KAIJA

I CAN'T BELIEVE I spoke to Mack that way. I was in defense mode and it just popped out of my mouth. I clench my jaw as I follow Anderson into school. I hid out with him all Sunday, hoping not to bump into the star quarterback. Mack Mahoney has an unnerving effect on me. He's so sexy, yet arrogant…full of himself, but there's something in his eyes that tells me it's all for show.

As much as I want to figure him out, I won't go there. My snarky comments after the game (although said somewhat in jest) are simply proof that the guy brings out the worst in me. I've no doubt made an enemy of Colt and his sweet little girlfriend Tori, as well.

Sigh.

I shouldn't be sighing. I should be happy.

I don't want to be part of that crowd. After how rude I was, I'm sure I've put them all off.

So why can't I get over this biting disappointment?

"Do you remember where your classes are for the morning?" Anderson distracts me with his question.

"Uh." I blink, slow to process it, then nod and force a smile. "Uh-huh. I'm good. Plus, I can always ask for directions if I get lost, right?"

Anderson gives me a kind smile. I can tell by the tightening in the corners of his eyes that he was kind of hoping I'd ask him to stick with me and show me around, but I spent the whole day with him yesterday and quickly discovered he's the kind of guy that's way more likable in small bursts. There's only so much general knowledge I can handle in one day.

"Did you know that…?"

Ugh. I was fighting a serious case of snarky backchat by the afternoon. I had a feeling Anderson wouldn't cope with my contemptuous teasing as well as Mack did. If anything, Mack looked like he enjoyed it.

Yet another reason to like him…and another reason to stay as far away from him as possible.

I don't need any excuses to play my mean girl routine.

"Well, enjoy your first Monday." Anderson tentatively pats my shoulder, then waves his long fingers at me.

I smile back and wave, then head for my locker. I don't have much time before the bell, but I forgot my notepad on Friday—thanks to Mack distracting me—and I want to re-read my U.S. government stuff before class. Hopefully I won't be so lost today.

Busting around the corner, I duck and weave through student traffic until I reach my locker. I actually pass it and have to backtrack three metal doors before finding it. Punching in my combination, I swing open the door and let out a loud scream.

There's a humongous, hairy spider dangling in front of my books.

This thing is a mother, with vibrating legs and red, beady eyes.

Pressing my hand into my belly, I expel my breath, my racing heart stumbling back into rhythm as logic kicks in and tells me it's a fake.

A smile tugs at my lips. Reaching for the spider, I unhook it and show the concerned citizens around me that it was just a prank. A few of the girls start muttering OMGs and saying they could never cope with that.

I have three older brothers. A fake spider in my locker is child's play.

I mean, my heart is still pounding like crazy, but I'm not about to show anyone how close to the verge of fainting I got. Whoever played this prank is not going to get that kind of satisfaction from me.

Glancing around, I scan the halls and spot Mack leaning against the wall at the end of one. His handsome face rises with a playful grin.

I narrow my eyes at him and shake my head, wishing like crazy that my mouth would control itself and stop smiling! I should be seriously pissed right now, but all I want to do is burst out laughing and yell, "Nice one, dickhead."

It's as if Mack can read my mind. His sexy mouth blooms into a full grin, and then he has the balls to give me a two-fingered salute.

I cock my eyebrow.

Challenge accepted, mate. You better watch your back.

Squeezing the spider in my hand, I smirk at him and enjoy the twinkle in his eye as he snickers and saunters out of view. I throw the spider into my locker and pull out my notes from Friday. The bell starts to ring as I slam my locker shut and head to class. My mind is racing with ideas of how to get Mack back, each one sending a sizzling sparkle right through my center.

I shouldn't be reacting this way. After everything I went through in New Zealand, I should be ignoring the spider. But it's a funny prank, and unlike my jerk ex-boyfriend, Mack only did it for a laugh.

I can't fight my smile as I picture his cocky little salute. His brown gaze had been bright and playful, not narrowed and sinister.

He isn't out to hurt me...get my back up, maybe, but not take me down. I'm pretty sure I can tell the difference, which is why I'm also pretty sure that I won't be able to resist getting him back.

9

THE PRANK BACK

MACK

KAIJA'S REACTION to my spider prank yesterday was just what I expected. Seeing her fight that smile and then grin at me with a challenging glint in her eye told me everything I needed to know.

Whether she wants to be or not, she's the girl for me… and things are going to get interesting.

I was on high alert for retribution all of Monday, but nothing ever came. I then vacillated between confidence in Kaija taking my prank well and wanting to play to thinking, *I went too far and killed my chances.*

I can't tell you how good it felt to get into my Camaro on Tuesday afternoon and have it start acting up. I punched the gas and a loud whistle sounded. I jerked to a stop and looked at my dashboard, the offending whistling making my forehead wrinkle.

"What the hell is that?" Layla's pretty face scrunches with a frown.

I snicker and scan the dials and electronics, convinced Kaija is behind this. "Not sure."

I gently accelerate toward the school exit and the whistle hits a crescendo.

"Seriously. What is wrong with your car?" Layla's voice pitches with a small touch of fear. Not many people would ever notice it, but I'm hyper aware. She's basically been scared of her own shadow since Dad died. She's really good at hiding it, but her veneer is paper-thin when you've watched her try—and fail—to process the loss of her greatest hero. I've attempted to fill the space as best I can, but it's hard. I'll never be my father and, like I said before, it's damn hard living up to his epic legacy.

I give her a reassuring smile and pat her jean-clad knee. "It's all good, Lay-lay. I'm guessing it's just a prank."

"Who would prank *you*?"

A broad smile stretches across my face.

Pulling to the curb, I jump out and walk around the car, trying to figure out what Kaija's done. I have to admire the fact she's had the balls to mess with my car. This thing is my pride and joy. Dad handed me the keys on my twelfth birthday and told me the day I turned sixteen, it was all mine. I wish he could have been there to see me drive his beloved Camaro for the first time.

The whistling noise is fading as I wander around the back of the car, but I'm pretty sure it'll start up again the second I hit the gas.

"Gutsy move, Kiwi Girl." It only makes me like her more. She isn't afraid of anything.

Colt pulls up behind me and gets out of his truck with Finn on his tail.

"What's up, bro?" Finn lifts his chin at me.

"Not sure." I scratch the back of my head. "My car's doing this whistling thing."

"Yeah, we can hear that." Colt gives me a teasing grin before crouching low and looking for the cause of the noise.

The passenger door opens and slams shut. Layla stalks around the car, her arms crossed as she scowls at my blue and orange baby. The guy who owns the paint shop was good friends with my dad and had the car painted midnight blue with orange racing stripes for my birthday last year. Mom was so excited, she nearly peed herself when Martin pulled off the white sheet to reveal my *new* car. I didn't have the heart to tell them that I kind of liked the original grey-steel paint job.

"Have you figured it out yet?" Layla's tone is still laced with worry. I can't decide if she's more concerned for the safety of my car or her reputation. People are slowing down as they drive out of school, checking out the situation.

I wave my hand at one offer of help, shaking my head with a "Thanks, anyway."

Layla glances over her shoulder before shuffling closer to us, hiding herself from view in front of Finn. He glances down at her, his lips pursing. It's no secret he's not Layla's biggest fan. He's never rude to her or anything, but his quiet looks of disapproval are enough. If I asked him to, he'd protect her at any cost, but that doesn't mean he has to like her.

Colt starts laughing and points to the back of my car. "I think I've found the problem."

I bob down beside him and grin. A whistle has been slotted into my exhaust pipe and duct-taped into place. "Nice move, Kiwi Girl."

"She did that?" Finn's eyebrows flicker as he moves to turn off the ignition.

Layla's high boots click into view. "How are you so sure?"

I squint up at her. "Because I left a fake spider in her locker yesterday."

A loud laugh pops out of Finn's mouth while Layla's upper lip curls. I stand tall to look down at her. "What?"

"Why would you go pranking her?"

I can't help a smirk as I shrug and try to play it down.

She rolls her eyes. "Why mess with the new girl? Don't you think it's a little mean?"

"It's not mean." I point down at my exhaust while Colt unwinds the tape and pulls the whistle free. "She obviously wants to play."

"Don't mess with fire, Mack. You need to stick with your people." Layla flicks a lock of sleek hair over her shoulder like a snotty-nosed princess.

A sharp frown dents my features. "What is it with this 'your people' crap? You've been hanging out with Roxy too long."

Her gaze shifts to the ground, a red hue burning her pale cheeks. "You know what I mean."

"Yeah, I know exactly what you mean...and I think it's bullshit. You girls need to get over yourselves."

She doesn't say anything, just shrugs and clips back to

the car. I glance at Finn, who's gazing after her with an unimpressed frown.

"I hate this, man." I spread my arms wide. "Why do the lines have to be drawn in the first place?"

"You don't have to tell me." Finn rubs his short Afro curls and glances at the whistle Colt's holding. "She's on point with one thing, though. Do you really want to mess with the new girl?"

"Yeah, man." Colt throws me the whistle. "It's not like we're in the third grade anymore. You don't have to be mean to get her attention."

"Hey, I tried the conventional method and it didn't fly." I tuck the whistle into my pocket. "Besides, gentleman, she retaliated…and she wouldn't have done that if she didn't want to play."

My chest buzzes with giddy anticipation as my mind starts burning with ways to pay her back. Oh man, I am going to enjoy this.

10

THE SAMMY ALLIANCE

KAIJA

I HIDE around the edge of the main school building, watching Mack scratch the back of his head and chat with his friends. Much to my disappointment, they found the whistle easily and Mack didn't seem flustered at all. I'd seen him lovingly touch his car as he walked around it after school yesterday. He was probably one of those guys who didn't let you put your feet on the dashboard and who got off on washing it every weekend. But from the glimpses of his face I managed to catch, he almost looked pleased that someone had tampered with it.

Which meant only one thing.

He knew it was me. I guess I should have seen that one

coming. Of course I was going to pay back the spider scare; I practically shouted it at him when we were playing eye-flirt yesterday morning.

Because of his whole *I love, and most likely name, my car* thing, I was hoping for a little panic and frustration. But bloody hell, he looked triumphant!

Why?

No, I don't want to answer that question, which means I should seriously stop playing this game.

Retaliating, although fun, has obviously pleased him. And as handsome as his face is in this light—the curve of his lip at the corner, the way his chin dimple pops in and out of place while his square-cut jaw flexes—I should really back off now or…

"So, do you come here often?"

The soft question jerks me around and I find myself face-to-face with a tomboy wearing the best smirk I've ever seen. It's like she was born to do it or something. *How to make smirking look good by Samantha Carmichael.*

She's straddling a beat-up looking BMX, her long hair pulled into a messy braid over her shoulder. A tatty baseball cap is backwards on her head, and her ripped jeans and scuffed Converse have my lips forming a smirk of their own.

"Sam, right? We're neighbors at the moment."

"That we are." She sticks out her hand. "We haven't officially met yet, but if you're the chick responsible for the whistle in Mack-Attack's exhaust pipe, then I'm very pleased to meet you."

An instant grin pops my lips wide. I reach for her hand and give it a firm shake. "Glad you enjoyed it."

She points into the parking area. "I think anyone leaving school right now enjoyed it."

I peek over my shoulder and watch the mix of gazes aimed at the football boys. Anderson and his crew are snickering behind their hands while some of the cheer girls bustle through the crowd to try to find out what's going on.

"So, where'd you come up with the idea?" Sammy grips the handlebars as I spin back to face her.

"Oh, that?" I point over my shoulder with my thumb. "One of my brothers did it to his most despised teacher a couple of years ago."

Sammy laughs—a low, husky chuckle. "That's savage. I like him already."

A swift breeze whistles between us, blowing a clump of hair into my face. I tuck the locks behind my ear and pull the loose strands off my lips. They feel kind of dry, no doubt missing the gloss they've grown accustomed to over the last few years. In a bid to make a dramatic change, I'm going makeup free. It's taking a major adjustment on my part, but I can't bend. I came here to be someone different. I'm not allowed to be anal about my appearance anymore. Basically I'm avoiding the mirror at all costs. And that's a huge deal, believe me.

"So, what are you going to do next?" Sammy's question distracts me.

"I guess I kind of have to wait for him to get me back first."

Sammy nods. "He won't take long."

"Yeah, I know." I shrug.

Sammy's eyes narrow as she scrutinizes my expression. "You've had experience with guys like him before, haven't you?"

I flash her a quick look of warning, which she picks up immediately. Perceptive girl.

Her brow crinkles before she shows off her smirk again. "To be honest, I really couldn't give a shit what your deal is, but I do love the idea of guys who think they're *all that* getting pranked. If you need any ideas, or help, count me in."

"Really?" I cross my arms and tip my head to study her.

She chuckles. "I'm always up for that kind of thing. In fact, if you really want to make an impression, I've got a great idea."

A smile tugs at my lips, and against my better judgment I lean forward and ask, "What are you thinking?"

11

CUPCAKE, ANYONE?

MACK

BEFORE I STARTED my first year at Nelson Middle School, my dad gave me a piece of advice: Get in good with the office staff and the janitor. You treat them well and they'll help you out whenever you need it. So I took it onboard...and that is why I am able to respond to Kaija's whistle prank so swiftly.

"Thanks so much, Larry." I pat the janitor on the shoulder as he opens Kaija's locker.

"Just make sure you're done before anyone gets here," he grumbles.

I look at my watch. "School doesn't start for an hour. I should be good."

"And this has to be the last time, Mahoney. You're just lucky she didn't question how you got into her locker last time."

"Yeah, yeah, I know. This'll be the last locker one, I promise."

Larry's beady brown eyes stare me down. "You sure you want to be doing this? There's better ways to get a girl's attention, you know? Your dad won over your mother in more ordinary ways, if you get my drift."

I grin. "This girl is anything but ordinary. Trust me, I know what I'm doing."

"Hmmmm." He gives me a reluctant nod before walking off, his shoes squeaking on the polished floor while the keys on his belt jangle a tune.

Yanking the stuff out of my backpack, I quickly set to work.

Forty-five minutes later, I ease Kaija's locker closed, then hurry down the hall to wait for her. Taking up my post like I did last time, I watch her stroll down the hall, chatting with Anderson. As usual, he's prattling on about something. Kaija's eyes tighten at the corners and her lips form a closed-mouth smile. She looks around, pursing her lips and nodding. Man, she's so beautiful. I love the richness of her hair and the way it falls over her shoulders like a lush, silk blanket. The first time I introduced myself, I was standing close enough to score a whiff—watermelons. She smelled like watermelon shampoo. And don't even get me started on her skin. It looks soft and creamy, probably tastes just as sweet. Unlike most of the girls in this school, she doesn't wear any makeup. None that I can tell, anyway. She doesn't really need it, if you ask me, but I do find it puzzling. Girls of her caliber, kind of like my sister, somehow feel the need to amp it up with makeup, and I'm surprised Kaija hasn't gone that way too.

She's such a complex blend—she oozes the feisty coolness that Roxy and Layla have, but it's like she's trying to hide it or something. I don't know. I'm probably talking out my butt. All I do know is that she has me curious, desperate to know more.

Anderson stops at his locker, still talking. As soon as his door opens and he's out of view, Kaija rolls her eyes and tips her head to the ceiling. I grin at her expression, my heart starting to race as she unlocks her locker and flips it open. She jerks still, her lips parting for a second before she reaches inside and pulls out one of her aluminum foil-wrapped books. Running her fingers over it, she ducks her head into the small space and is now realizing that every single thing in her locker has been lovingly wrapped in foil, I even found a pencil case in there and took the time to wrap each item inside it.

Her head pops back into view, her parted lips finally rising into a broad smile. She fights the grin, her nose wrinkling before she spins to find me.

I wave at her, showing off my cheesiest smile.

Her eyes narrow and she flips me the bird. I start laughing, which makes her eyes narrow into fine slits.

"Have a nice day, Kiwi Girl!" I call down the hallway before sauntering off to class.

I half expect her to shout out some snarky response, but she doesn't say anything, and I don't want to lose the impact of my cool walkaway by turning around.

All I have to do now is wait for her next prank.

———

She doesn't prank back.

I waited all Wednesday, and Thursday, but she never bit. What the hell? I didn't think the foil wrap was that bad. I thought she'd keep playing.

I stalk the halls on Friday morning, wondering what I'm supposed to do next. I can't prank her again, not without her getting me first. But we're about to take a week off for Thanksgiving, and I doubt I'll get many opportunities then. I mean, I could use Roxy as an excuse to swing past the Fosters' place, but that would be a totally dick move on my part. I'm not into stringing girls along; I like to be upfront and open. Roxy and I have made out at a few bonfires before, but she knows I don't think of her like a girlfriend. We just like to have a little fun together, that's all.

Thoughts of Thanksgiving turn my unsettled insides to black ash. Derek's staying this holiday. Kill me now. It'll be impossible for Layla and me to relax with that jerk in the house. The worst part is that Trevor, his brother, isn't even going to be there. As soon as he found out it was Martin's turn to have them, he bailed and said he'd rather stay studying on the East Coast. Yeah, he's got issues with his old man—hates the guy for leaving his mother. Anyway, he goes to some high-brow college. I can't remember which one. The point is that out of the two brothers, he's the nicer one…and without him there, Derek's going to be at full-force.

He's one of those two-faced assholes who puts on a show for his dad and my mother. Mom thinks he's amazing and sweet and doesn't understand why I'm so surly around him. But as soon as her back is turned, Derek's claws come out. He's a manipulative douchebag. As if losing my father wasn't bad enough, having to follow up that shit-storm with a life with Derek Wiseman is the most brutal blow of all.

"Mack Mahoney, could you please come to the office?" Mrs. Trillman's voice squawks out of the loud speakers.

My brow wrinkles, but I turn for the office. It's not like I've done anything to get in trouble. There's no way Larry would have squealed on me about Kaija's locker, and I'm ninety-nine percent certain Kaija wouldn't, either.

The lunch bell's about to ring, so maybe the principal wants me to do something. Whenever a student is needed to make the school look good, he always calls on me. I was interviewed over the weekend about our big win—maybe another reporter's here for some follow-up comments.

Swinging the glass door open, I walk into the office and am greeted by the two smiling office ladies.

"Hi, Mack." Mrs. Trillman's smile is on full-beam. She's like the sweetest lady on the planet, and totally reminds me of my dad's mother. One of those round, cheery-faced ladies who always makes you feel important.

"Hey, Mrs. T. How's it going?"

"Great. Thank you, hon." She places a large box on the counter. I recognize the packaging immediately and can't help a smile—Cupid's Bakery. Yes! I love that place. "This was delivered for you and the boys."

I reach for the envelope and rip it open.

. . .

To our favorite Raiders,

Congratulations on a great win. Here are some cupcakes to celebrate.

From your fans at Cupid's

"That's cool." I grin, showing her the note.

"Awww, how sweet. Well, you boys deserve it. Go and enjoy."

"Do you want one?" I go to open the box, but she stops me.

"Don't you dare tempt me with that chocolatey goodness. I'm trying to watch my weight."

"What are you talking about?" I beam at her. "You're gorgeous, Mrs. Trillman."

Her cheeks flash red. "Oh, stop it." She titters. "Go on, get going, before you make me blush some more."

I wink at her, setting off another round of giggles before taking the box and sauntering out of the office. Man, I love it when Cupid's surprises us like this. When we got into the division finals, they sent us three

Black Forest Chocolate Cakes that were out of this world. They are by far the best bakery in town.

With a smug smile, I saunter to the cafeteria with the massive box in my hands. The boys are going to love me for this. The open space is crowded with human traffic, so I lift the box high and make my way to the football table. As soon as I set the box down, I'm swamped.

Tyler flips the lid. The box is filled with cupcakes, made pretty with swirls of glossy, orange icing. "Yes! Damn, I love those guys."

"Not as much as I do, brother." Finn snags a cupcake and starts peeling off the wrapper.

I grab one before they're all taken, tearing the blue wrapper and shoving the whole thing in my mouth. I bite down, expecting to smile. Instead, my eyes bulge and my gag reflex kicks in.

Fire. Mint. Sour. Bitter—it's the most disgusting concoction I've ever tasted.

I spit the offending cupcake into my hand.

"What the f—?" Tyler starts hacking up the food while Finn pulls a series of ridiculous faces and forces himself to swallow...then lunges for the water bottle on the table and chugs.

In a mild state of shock, I scan the table of spluttering Raiders…and that's when I hear it.

A deep belly laugh. The kind people make when they can't control themselves.

I glance across the cafeteria and see a pair of sparkling emerald eyes staring back at me.

12

MUM + SKYPE = BUZZ KILL

KAIJA

SUBSTITUTE SUGAR FOR SALT, frosting for tooth-paste. Add three tablespoons of chili powder and enough food coloring to hide the evidence, and you have the most gag-worthy cupcakes on the market. Sammy's friends with the son of Cupid's Bakery's head baker, so he was able to score us the carton. She snuck the box into reception for me, and I wrote the note in my swirliest writing so no one could trace it back to me.

Too bad the sight of the coolest kids in school hacking like drama queens made me laugh so hard that I couldn't control the sounds coming out of my mouth.

Mack's eyes connect with mine and it only makes me

laugh harder. Sammy's beside me, her smile so broad it changes the whole shape of her face. She raises her hand and I slap it. We did good. It took us until after one in the morning, but it was worth it.

"Look at those faces." Sammy holds up her phone and starts clicking.

"Sammy!" Tyler hollers across the cafeteria, his long finger shaking. "You are so going to get it, girl."

"Bring it on, Mai Tai!" She hoots with laughter and keeps snapping pictures.

I look around and notice that Anderson and his friends are taking video footage. This thing could go viral.

The thought sobers me up for a quick second, but I don't have time to ponder the error of my ways. I'm locked in a silent convo with Mack, who is now wagging his finger at me and mouthing, "Just you wait."

He'll plan something epic for me over Thanksgiving, I just know it.

The biggest problem is, I kind of want him to, because the way he's looking at me right now...I can't get enough of it. Mack Mahoney's eyes on me are doing things they shouldn't.

But I want more.

Lunch ends up being a raucous affair with catcalls across the cafeteria. Some of the guys are steamed, others are laughing. It doesn't take them long to form a huddle.

"They're plotting their revenge already," Sammy whispers in my ear.

I snicker.

"We'll have to get together over the break and make sure we have a counter-attack in place. Ooooo, this is going to be fun!" She winks at me. "I'm liking you, Kiwi Girl. Hope you stick around."

I don't have the heart to tell her I'll be gone in less than three months, back to stinky old New Zealand and a world of problems I don't want to face. Sammy practically skips away from me, swinging by the table to say something that has Tyler throwing a cupcake at her. She dodges it with a laugh and starts running when he picks up another one and chases after her.

My gaze locks with Mack's again, his cheeky smirk enough to make my insides buzz.

This is a bad idea, Kai. You're playing with fire.

I force my eyes away from his, knowing the truth but not wanting to listen. Hanging out with Sam, plotting our revenge—heck, even unwrapping all my school stuff on Wednesday—was fun. I mean, it was a total pain in the butt, but every time I tore at that foil, I thought of Mack taking the time to do it…and that made me kind of warm on the inside.

Would it really be so bad to let him in while I'm here?

I snap my eyes shut, forcing my mind away from the question. But it doesn't want to be forced away. It wants to play with the idea, let it linger.

The bell makes me flinch. I snatch my stuff and stand, knocking into Anderson. He gives me a closed-mouth smile and looks as though he wants to say something, then shakes his head. I don't press him, partly because I don't want to have to walk with him to class…and also because he'll no doubt have something incredibly mature to say. Something that will put me in my place and remind me how childish I'm being.

"I'll catch you later." I take off to class and after school catch the bus home with Dana. She goes on and on about the dramatic events in the cafeteria, obviously unaware that Sammy was simply an accomplice. Skater girl wouldn't have bothered with such an elaborate prank if she hadn't been trying to help me out.

I let Dana think what she likes. I'm not up for telling her the truth. She'll want to know why I was playing this game with Mack, and I don't want to explain it out loud. I barely understand it myself. I'm supposed to be *avoiding* guys like him, but after only one week I am immersed in a prank war that I'm enjoying way too much to quit.

Dana follows me into the house and would have followed me upstairs too if Mrs. Foster hadn't stopped us in the entrance.

"Welcome home, girls." She grins. "Kaija, your mom just tried to call you on Skype. I promised her I'd get you to call back as soon as you got home."

"Oh, thanks." I force a smile and trudge up to my room, dread already roiling in my stomach.

Mum doesn't want me here. She didn't want her baby girl flying halfway around the world to attend a school she knew nothing about. Mr. Foster is an acquaintance of my dad's from ages ago—they studied together at Auckland University for one semester and then kept in touch. He's been offering to have us stay for years. We managed one trip when I was four—totally can't remember it, and it was the basis of my argument when I changed my mind and decided to come. Dad was an easy sell, but Mum was something else.

Opening up my laptop, I mentally prepare for another taxing conversation. Mum doesn't know all the details of why I chose to run. She knows parts and has made all her own assumptions. Most of them are wrong, but I don't have it in me to tell her the truth. Because she'll never look at me the same again.

The Skype beeps and sings and then starts ringing.

"Hello? Hello, Kaija?" Her voice is so high and hopeful.

"Hey, Mum."

Her pixelated face comes clear, her hazel eyes zeroing in on me. I look at the round curve of her cheeks and the thick locks of hair framing her face. She's getting wrinkle lines around her eyes when she smiles now.

"How's my baby girl?"

"I'm doing good." I nod. "It's been a great first week. People are really…" I smile. "Nice, interesting."

"Well, that's great. I'm glad you're adjusting so easily." Her voice and face are saying different things.

I force a sweet tone and really try to sell it. "Yep, I am. So glad I made the decision to come. This is a really good experience for me."

The wrinkle lines are more marked when she's forcing a smile. "We miss you."

"I know, Mum. You put that in every email."

"Well, the house is quiet without you! Corbin's hardly

ever here, either. Now that uni's finished he's off at the beach all day. We barely see him anymore."

"I know you miss your babies, Mum."

"Empty nest doesn't suit me, Kai. It really doesn't."

"I'll be back soon. Just think of this as good practice."

Mum makes a face and whines in her throat, her perceptive eyes trying to read my face through Skype. "You sure you're happy?"

"Yes." I bulge my eyes at her. "This is going to be the best three months I've ever had."

"I doubt that," she mumbles. Her dark eyebrows dip together and then rise as she changes the subject. "Hanson popped over yesterday to see how you were doing. Are you not keeping in touch? I thought he was your boyfriend."

My blood flashes icy cold and I swallow. "We kind of broke up before I left."

Mom's eyes narrow. "It wasn't because of…?"

"No." The shake of my head is too adamant, too furious. I force my neck to stop moving and go for a half-truth. "Things have been falling apart for a while, and I just thought breaking up before I left was the right move."

"He doesn't seem to think so. He said that he and Anna are really missing you. I thought you'd be posting your news to them on Facebook or something."

Thankfully for me, my mother is technologically retarded, so she's never really gotten into social media. None of her children have encouraged her to, either. I guess it's kind of selfish, but it's saved our lives, believe me!

"I don't want to spend my time here on the computer. I've been…busy, getting to know people. I haven't really been online much."

Truth: I haven't touched social media since I ran crying to Hanson about *what happened with Eloise,* and he then blabbed to Anna who used it against me. They were both trying to protect their own asses and not come off like the guilty ones. So they reverted all blame to me and started a frenzy of posts on Facebook and Twitter… Then they flooded Instagram with cartoon depictions of what went down. I was so horrified I've basically stayed offline since. I don't want to know what people are saying about me.

"Well, I thought it was nice that he wanted to check in." Mom smiles.

For someone who seems so insightful, sometimes she's completely blind.

Yeah, right! Nice? The only reason he popped over was

to get more goods for the gossip train Anna sent screaming out of the station. I wouldn't be surprised if she'd sent him to do her dirty work. Their betrayal tastes bitter, and it takes everything in me not to curl my lip at the mention of my ex-boyfriend and best friend. The fact that they didn't show any kind of remorse over what happened is testament to the jerks they both are. Instead of shouldering some of the blame, they made sure all fingers were pointing directly at me.

Mom distracts me with another bone-chilling revelation. "I called the Cochrans last week. Eloise is back home now."

My already icy blood makes a beeline for my brain, making it hard to see straight.

"Oh, yeah?" I can't keep the shake from my voice.

"She still has to go back in for regular checks and they'll be monitoring her closely, but I thought it was encouraging that she can be back home with her family again. It's been a rough time."

I swallow, images of her ghostly white skin and limp body torturing me.

"Yeah, that is good."

"Maybe you should try contacting her. You two used to be inseparable when you were kids. She could probably use a friend right now. The fact she did it in your…"

"Can we not talk about it, please?"

Mum sighs, her expression a mixture of compassion and concern. "You're going to need to at some point, Kai."

My insides start to tremble as tears sting my eyes. My nose is tingling and if I don't end the call soon, a loud, wretched sob is going to burst out of my mouth. "Not to be rude, but I have to go. Um, I just heard Mrs. Foster calling. I think we're going out for dinner tonight, so I need to get ready."

"Oh, okay." Mum can probably see straight through my lie.

As her eyes start to narrow, I flash her my best smile. "I love you, Mum."

Her expression turns to mush and she tips her head. "Love you so much, baby girl. I miss you."

"Don't worry. I'll be home before you know it."

"You take care."

"Give Dad a kiss for me, okay?"

"You bet."

I hang up before more can be said. Slapping my laptop

shut, I slam back into my seat and force air in through my nose.

A few hours ago, I was flirting with Mack Mahoney, completely forgetting about life back in New Zealand. Or the life that nearly wasn't, because of me.

My purpose for coming here was to escape what I'd done.

To make a change.

To *not* fall back into the life I was once living...and what had I done so far?

Started a dangerous game with the hottest guy in school, basically the American version of Hanson.

"You're an idiot," I whisper. "Stupid girl." I slam my teeth together and fight the burning tears.

My phone buzzes with a text. I pull it out of my pocket and check the screen.

Got the best idea. Come over when you can and we'll work out the details.

Sam

Swiping my finger right, I press the X and ignore the text. I won't be doing any more pranks.

I just lost focus there for a second, but Mum's call has brought it all back again.

I'm not the girl who flirts with flames anymore.

I have to disengage and be the girl I'm supposed to be.

The one who doesn't hurt innocent people.

13

DICKMAN AT HIS BEST

MACK

EVERY TIME I think about Kaija and Sammy's prank, a smile pops onto my face. The only thing to kill it is Derek and his smarmy, punchable face. He stares at me across the Thanksgiving table, chewing his turkey leg with a dark glint in his eye. I can't even begin to explain how much it sucks having Dickman as a step-brother. He arrived on Saturday to spend the entire week with us. It's been hell.

Mom and Martin have forced us to spend 'quality time' together. Are they really that stupid? Or do they just not want to believe the angst simmering below the surface? It doesn't help that Derek is the expert at putting on a show. With my mom, he's attentive and sweet, articulate and kind.

Truth: The guy's a two-faced asshole who is hell-bent on making me look bad.

Mom looks at us and smiles brightly. "Who's enjoying the turkey? Is it okay? Did I cook it alright?"

I force a smile, about to tell her it's great, when Dickman talks over me. "Celia, it's amazing. Truly."

"Thank you, sweetheart." Her nose wrinkles as she turns her smile from her stepson to her husband. They share one of those *this is working* kind of looks. Pretending that the whole blended family thing is a piece of cake. They're too in love to think anything else.

Derek shoots me a greasy smile before turning it on Layla, who shrinks away from him. Keeping her eyes down, she punctures a morsel of potato and nibbles it off the end of her fork.

"So, the game starts in twenty minutes. Who's ready to see the Packers beat the Lions?" Martin's eyes land on me, full of hope and expectation. He probably wants me to engage in some kind of friendly banter so he can start up a rousing speech about why the Green Bay Packers are the best team in the NFL.

Not gonna happen.

So I just nod. "Yep."

Mom's lips flatline, her forehead wrinkling at my serious lack of effort.

"Who knows, son. You might be playing for 'em one of these days."

Martin's jolly words make my shoulders snap tight. They also narrow Derek's gaze to laser slits that I can feel burning my forehead. "Yeah, star quarterback," he says. "Wow. You so deserve that."

I clench my jaw at Derek's scathing tone, then wonder if my teeth will crack when his father goes on to make it a million times worse.

"You'll get your chance, Derek. A college is going to pick you up in the new year. You just wait and see. We all have to acknowledge that Mack's had a better season than you." He beams at me.

"Minus the angry incident," Mom mutters.

Yeah, my teeth are definitely going to crack. When's she going to let that go already?

So I punched the guy on the field...like weeks ago. Big deal. His friend had just monster-smashed Colt in the ribs, pulling our playmaker out for a whole week. The move was illegal and I *knew* it had been Derek's idea.

He's been playing the sympathy card ever since.

Derek makes a face and Mom's expression melts into an apologetic frown.

I roll my eyes and share a quick look with Layla. Thank God there's one person at the table who understands.

"You accepted the offer from Boise State yet?" Martin slathers his forkful of turkey with cranberry sauce. "Your dad's gonna be so proud."

My dad's not here to feel proud. He's dead, remember? You're sitting in his chair right now!

I don't say any of the words bellowing in my brain. Instead, I swallow back my vicious tone and mumble, "Signing day's not until February, so I still have some time." I spin the fork in my fingers.

"Of course you're going to sign, though." Mom grins. "We've talked about this. Following in your father's footsteps is…" Her voice grows soft as her eyes start to glisten. "Martin's right. Dad will be so proud of you."

Her husky words feel like a mallet, slamming into my shoulders and pummeling me to the ground. How can I tell her that maybe I don't want to play football for the rest of my life? That maybe I want to be my own man and not have the burden of following in my father's epic footsteps?

Martin reaches for her hand, rubbing it with his thumb and giving her a tender smile. She squeezes his fingers and sniffs, pulling herself together. It's no secret how much she loved my dad, but I can't help wondering if she loves Martin more. They're so wrapped up in each other...like lovesick teens or something.

My thoughts shift to Kaija and her green eyes. Is this how Martin feels when he looks at my mom?

"I'm done." Layla dumps her napkin on the table and rises from her seat. "Great meal, Mom. Thanks."

"Wait, sweetie, I haven't excused you. We're having a family—"

"I'm excusing myself." Layla's gaze skims Mom's fingers wrapped around Martin's hand. "Football doesn't really interest me, so..."

"What about the peach cobbler your mom made? I know you won't want to miss that." Martin's smile is strained, his cheeks taut as he tries to keep it in place.

"I don't like peaches. That's *your* favorite," she tells him. Her eyes dart to Mom's mottled face.

Derek's lips rise with a smirk as the two women engage in a silent standoff. Mom's eye-bulging and subtle head tips have zero effect. My little sister pastes on a cheesy smile and flounces out of the room.

"Layla, get back here!" Mom goes to rise from her seat but Martin stops her.

"Honey, it's okay. She's still adjusting."

"We've been together for three years, Martin. She's had long enough to adjust. I hate the way she talks to you."

Martin shrugs. "At least she's not openly rude."

Mom rolls her eyes. "I wish she could be more like Derek."

Bile swirls in my stomach, bitter and acidic. Mom smiles at Dickman and reaches over to pat his hand. "I did very well to score you and Trevor as stepsons."

Her sweet words fall flat and unbelievable into the room.

We all know what a joke that sentiment is. Trevor's forfeited the holidays because of her.

"Thanks, Celia. That means a lot."

Bullshit. He doesn't mean that. Can she honestly not see the fake, plastic glint in his eyes right now?

Martin and my mom go back to looking at each other like the outside world doesn't exist.

Dickman and I go back to chomping our food and sending each other evil glares that would have us dead on the floor in seconds. If looks could kill, right?

I cut into my turkey and force my mind back to Kaija. She's the only thing keeping me sane these holidays. If

I'm not dreaming about her gorgeous face and feisty smile...or that cute belly laugh, I'm coming up with ways to prank her. I can't wait to see the look on her face when me and some of the guys follow through on the idea Tyler came up with yesterday.

My lips curve with a quick grin that not even Derek can kill this time.

The fact that his forehead wrinkles with a curious frown only makes it that much better.

Like I'm ever going to tell him about Kaija Bennett.

14

RADIO SILENCE

KAIJA

WE DON'T CELEBRATE Thanksgiving in New Zealand, so the whole holiday was a new experience for me. It was actually really cool. I love the idea of celebrating a day where we can focus solely on being grateful. When the extended Foster family went around the table and all had to say something they were thankful for, all I could think about was Mack. It was totally crazy, because I am not grateful for Mack at all!

In the end, I mumbled some lame-ass line like, "I'm grateful for the Fosters taking me in and being so kind."

I got a bunch of smiles and head tips, and then one auntie made everyone laugh by saying how adorable my accent was. The house was jam-packed for three full days, and by Sunday afternoon I was exhausted. There are only so many questions you can answer *repeatedly* about your country.

In saying that, it was the perfect excuse to ignore Sammy's texts. She tried three times before finally giving up. I did feel bad for treating her that way, but I didn't know what else to do. Radio silence seemed the best course of action.

I keep telling myself this lie as I walk into school on Monday morning, scanning the halls for the skater girl. She's going to be pissed off with me. Sammy's not the kind of girl to be meek and mild about this sort of stuff. She'll challenge me on my behavior, and I need to be ready with a credible answer.

"So, maybe this weekend?" Anderson stares down at me, all expectant.

"Huh?" I frown.

"I knew you weren't listening." He rolls his eyes and nudges me with his shoulder. "Do you want to go to the museum on Saturday?"

"Oh, yeah. That history display thing."

"The Idaho Military Museum. It'll take us about three hours to drive there, but it'll be totally worth it."

I remind myself that his beaming smile is what I'm supposed to want. I should be jumping all over his invitation. It'll get me out of Nelson for a day and quite possibly help me stop thinking about Mack. Anderson's the type of person who will bring out the boring—I mean, the best in me.

I force a smile and bob my head. "Sounds cool."

"Awesome." He grins even wider, his square teeth looking like rows of white Juicy Fruit gum. "Well, I'm gonna go and catch up with Amy in the library. I'll see you at lunch time."

"Sounds good." I wave at him and head for my locker. My eyes narrow as I approach my small space, wondering what kind of surprise I'm going to find. Whatever it is, I can't react to it.

Scanning the hall, I notice Mack down the end. He flashes me a friendly smile, tipping his chin at me before disappearing around the corner. I frown, wondering why he's not staying to watch.

Cautiously unlocking the door, I open it and am amazed to find absolutely nothing wrong.

No wonder he didn't stay to watch.

Unzipping my bag, I pull out the heavy textbook I lugged home and then promptly ignored all holiday.

"I see you're still here."

The sharp voice makes me turn. I rest the book against

my hip and eye up the dazzling brunette in front of me. Roxanne Carmichael. What the hell does she want?

I arch my eyebrow, putting on the kind of face that makes other girls feel inferior—the kind Roxy is an expert at. "Was I supposed to be somewhere else?"

She checks her nails—a standard *I don't give a shit about you* tactic. I used to do it all the time. Her big hoop earrings sway as she flicks her perfect curls over her slender shoulder. "I just thought you may have returned to Hobbit land over the break, especially since you went radio silent on my sister."

My eyes tighten at the corners, the only sign of remorse I'm willing to show her. "Sorry to disappoint."

She waves her hand in the air and hitches her right shoulder. "Don't worry about it. I can handle a little foreign matter. I just hope you can handle the heat."

I smirk. "The heat?"

She matches my look, her blue eyes sparking. "Those first few pranks were amateur, Kiwi Girl. The guys have had a whole week to come up with something epic. I'd watch my back if I were you. Mack's smarter than he looks, and no one ever gets away with shaming him like you've tried."

My jaw works to the side and I manage to force out a

short chuckle. "You know, if you're threatened by me, you should just come out and say it."

I expect her expression to flash with some kind of *you've got me* indicator. But she puts on this nonchalant pout and checks her nails again. "I'm not threatened. I'm just trying to be nice. In my world, girls stick together."

Another dig at the fact that I ditched her sister. I force my lips into a friendly smile. "Thanks, Roxy. That's really sweet."

"Well, don't say I didn't warn you."

Her fake smile matches mine and we play a quick game of pretend, saying sweet goodbyes and waving our fingers at each other. Her hips sway as she struts off. She manages to capture the eye of every drooling freshman the entire way down the hall.

For a quick second, I wonder if I don't know her as well as I think I do. Maybe she was trying to be nice and warn me that Mack might be after the long con.

No, surely not. That girl sends off all the cool vibes I used to parade around my school with. I know her type. I *was* her type. But not anymore...which is why I need to find her little sister and apologize.

It only takes me ten minutes. Sammy's locking up her bike with a thick chain and chunky-looking padlock.

"Hey, Sammy." I smile.

"Oh em gee, you're alive?" She puts on a surprised face…full of mockery.

That's okay. I deserve it. "I'm sorry, okay? I shouldn't have ignored you. I just changed my mind on the whole pranking thing and wasn't sure how to admit it."

She gives me a skeptical frown. "Seriously? That's so incredibly lame. Why are you giving up?"

I hesitate for a second, my mind scrambling. "I just… I don't want to get burned."

"Chicken." Sammy runs her long fingers through her hair and glares at me. I'm guessing that's the first brush her hair's had this morning. She's such a scruff, like the female version of my brother Corbin. I really hate that I can't get to know her better. She makes a clicking noise with her tongue as she looks away from me, obviously trying to hide her disappointment. "See, this is why I hang out with guys. They're decisive, honest, and uncomplicated."

I make a face and point my finger at her. "Don't you dare call me a princess."

"I won't, princess." She winks. "Such a bummer, though. I had some great ideas."

"You can still do them."

Her expression goes drier than the desert. "It only works because of the whole you and Mack thing. That's what makes it interesting."

I try not to openly balk, straining to keep my expression indifferent. "There's no me and Mack."

Sammy's *are you kidding me* face is comical. Her wide lips pull into this awkward smile while her eyebrows arch at the sides and dip into a V above her nose.

Thankfully, she picks up on my warning glare and her expression flatlines. She licks the edge of her mouth and nods. "Too bad. I think you'd look great together."

"No, we wouldn't." My voice comes out sounding like a squeak. "I... We aren't... It would never... I can't, okay? I just... I can't."

The smirk on Sammy's face is her best one yet. Her thin eyebrows arch even higher than they were before. "Wow. You must have one hell of a backstory."

The blood drains from my face. I can feel it rushing to my toes, like a torrent of obvious. Sammy's smirk falters, her expression softening to one of understanding. Her eyes narrow slightly as she tries to read me but then she straightens her shoulders and slaps me on the arm. "Well, good luck being boring, mate."

The way she emphasizes the word 'mate' cracks me up. Genuine laughter pops out of me, loud and refreshing.

She flashes me a quick grin and breezes past me. I watch her walk away and wonder if we'll ever hang out again. We only spent a short time together, but I really like her. After the way I ignored her, though, I can't imagine her investing much more time in me. It's probably for the best. I don't really deserve to make best friends with anyone ever again.

I *had* the world's best friend…and I shit all over her.

15

UNEXPECTED

MACK

THE BEAUTY of my next prank was a sweet addition Tyler and I added the day before school went back. Rather than getting Kaija on Monday, we decided to let her sweat it out and then lull her into a false sense of thinking *they must have given up on the pranking thing.*

So, all week I have been smiling at her, giving her the odd wave or just ignoring her completely when I pass her in the hallways. It's now Friday and the guys and I are lying in wait to pull off a prank that should make the most beautiful girl I know jump a mile. I'm secretly hoping that she'll scream, pat her chest or something, and then start laughing. I'll step into her space so she can lean on me, or hit me and tell me I'm a douchebag. I'll take the opportunity to rest my hand on that sexy little dip at the base of her spine before offering her a truce.

Hopefully we'll shake.

Hopefully the feel of our hands connecting will be enough to turn whatever we have into something more.

Is it insane to think one touch will be able to do that?

"Okay, here she comes." Tyler's voice is high with excitement as he hurries around the corner.

I grin at my other accomplices, Will and Darius, before pulling down my zombie mask and preparing for the ultimate surprise attack.

I tense, listening to the sound of footsteps in the hall, then quietly count, "Five, four, three, two, one, go!"

We jump out in unison, our arms raised and loud shouts bursting from our mouths.

As expected, Kaija screams. Her binder smacks to the floor and everyone around us starts laughing.

Except Kaija.

Totally unexpected is the stark fear in her eyes. It's not just a surprised flash; it's a lingering, painful horror. She stares at our masks like she's looking at a ghost or something. Her skin turns a sickly pale color.

I whip off my mask, my tousled hair probably looking

ridiculous. "Surprise!" I grin, trying to make the best of it.

It doesn't work. Her eyes don't even connect with mine. Instead, they rove the hallway, taking in the snickering faces before glancing back at the guys who are still masked up. Her face bunches with agony.

"Guys, take your masks off." I slap Tyler on the shoulder and smack Will's chest with the back of my hand.

They all start pulling off the ghoulish faces, but not before Kaija spins and makes a beeline for the exit.

"Kaija!" I snatch her binder off the floor and chase after her.

Damn, she's fast. She disappears around the next corner and by the time I get there, she's completely vanished.

"Which way did she go?" I ask a couple of freshmen. They both shrug and hurry away, my angry tone no doubt putting them off.

A sharp frown dents my forehead. My heart is racing.

Why did she look like that?

Why didn't she laugh and take it like she did all the other pranks?

An unsettling sickness tears at my guts. The guys bust around the corner.

"Where'd she go?" Will stops beside me.

Darius scans the hallway. "Geez, she took that well."

"Yeah, what's up with that?"

I glare at Tyler's question, hating that I don't know the answer. I thought the game we were playing was fun—a prank war that would lead to an epic backstory in our relationship.

But this has been a major backfire, and I have to find out why.

Scrunching the mask in my fist, I stalk away from my confused friends. Loping out of the school, I shove the mask into the first trashcan I pass and head for my car.

I should have Kaija by my side right now, finally agreeing to go on a date.

Instead, I'm skipping last period and heading home, feeling like the scum of the earth.

A FESTERING, ROTTING MASS

KAIJA

IT'S SATURDAY. I'm safe in my room at the Fosters' house, yet I'm completely haunted.

Seeing those masks jump out at me was like reliving my nightmare all over again.

Six weeks ago, when I got home from school, I found Eloise on my bed. She looked just like those zombies that scared me yesterday. Her face was pale, her eyes were open and red-rimmed. A little vomit dribbled from her mouth...and I thought she was dead.

I screamed, the exact same sound I made in the hallway when Mack tried to prank me. It traveled through my body like a sickness, ready to take me out. For a second, I froze, my eyes transfixed on the empty bottle of pills in Eloise's hand. Thankfully, the realization that she'd tried to commit suicide worked like an electric shock, jolting my body into action. I lurched for the phone, calling an ambulance before following the drill I'd been taught in PE class. I checked her pulse and found a soft, minimal beat in her neck, but she wasn't breathing. I did mouth-to-mouth until the ambulance arrived and took her away.

Then I went into a state of shock.

Her ghostly face has haunted me ever since.

Eloise and I grew apart when we were twelve. Before then, we'd been best mates...then her parents took her away to Myanmar. She started a new international school and I started at Macleans College. I thought it'd be terrifying without her, but I managed to get in with the cool crowd pretty quickly, and by the time Eloise returned two years later, I was immersed in a different world. There was no room for her.

She was the weird, out-of-touch, *foreign* kid and, as much as I wanted to pull her along with me, she just didn't fit.

So I cut her loose.

No, I did more than that.

I snap my eyes shut, hoping to escape the memories. But it doesn't work. It never does.

A soft knock at my door pulls me back to Nelson, Idaho.

"Come in," I croak.

The door eases open and Anderson's face appears. "Hey, you feeling okay?"

"Yep." I put on a brave smile. I've gotten good at that.

With a soft sigh, Anderson walks into my room and perches on the end of my bed. I'm sitting cross-legged by my pillow, spinning a pen in my hand. I've been attempting to write in my diary, but it's hard work today. I don't want to relive the hallway incident. But I'd been a religious diary-keeper since Eloise left me. At first, they were letters to her; we went old school and posted stuff, but then the letters were taking too long to go back and forth and I stopped wanting to share every graphic detail of my life...like how I got completely trashed at my first high school party...or how I let Brayden Wilder feel me up when we walked home from school one day...or how Anna and I skipped school to go shopping in New Market...or how I lost my virginity to Hanson way before I planned to.

Eloise would have disapproved of my new lifestyle, so I ended up writing for myself. I should burn the damn thing. The secrets inside will be the end of me. But old habits die hard, I guess. I've written a little about finding Eloise on my bed. I couldn't bring myself to write every detail…maybe that's one of the reasons it's plaguing me so bad. I haven't told anyone about the note she left, or the real effect seeing her almost die had on me. Those secrets remain within—a festering, rotting mass that will eventually eat me alive.

Mom's worried. She always tries to read into everything. She suggested counseling, but I refused it, saying it'd be more beneficial for me to get away to the States and have a change of scenery.

Yeah, right!

Rumors are running rife, of course, thanks to my ex-friends and social media, but no one will ever know the real truth.

I close my diary and slide it away in the bedside cabinet. I must hide it properly after Anderson leaves my room.

He shuffles a little closer, his long fingers splayed on my bedspread. "I'm really sorry Mack scared you like that. He's such an asshole."

Ah, the venomous tone. That's plain old jealousy right there.

My only response is a lame, closed-mouth smile.

Anderson's fingers glide further up the bed until they're resting just beneath my knee. His index finger pops up, tapping my jeans. "You know I'd never do that to you, right?"

What the hell is he doing?

I straighten my legs, stretching them out so his tentative hand is out of range. Running a hand through my hair, I smooth out my long locks and shake my head. "I'm okay, Anderson, really. You don't need to try to comfort me."

"I just heard you got a really big fright."

"Yeah, I bet the whole school was talking about it."

"Well, you did ditch last period. It must have been bad."

"I'm fine. Really." Another closed-mouth smile should do the trick.

Anderson grins back, moving a little closer and leaning down so our faces are aligned. "I love how tough you are. You don't let anyone beat you."

He doesn't know shit.

I am beaten. I've spent the last six weeks slowly disintegrating.

He touches my cheek, the pads of his fingers brushing against my skin.

"What are you doing?" I flick his hand off me.

"Oh." He jerks back, his cheeks burning so bright I think they might catch fire. "I just thought... Well, now that you've figured out that Mack's a total douche... I mean, I just thought that maybe we...could..." He swallows, his Adam's Apple looking large and pointy in his skinny neck. "Well, we are going on a date today and..."

"A date?" I frown. "I thought we were going to a museum?"

"We are. But it's the first time we've done anything just the two of us, and I figured..."

"Don't figure. Please, don't figure." I sigh. "Look, Andy, you're a nice guy and everything, but you're my host brother. *Brother*. You get what I mean? I don't see you as anything more."

His expression crumples.

Crap!

"Look, I'm sorry, okay? I don't want to hurt your feelings or anything. I just thought we were friends. I want to stay that way. Is that cool?"

"We just got along so well over Thanksgiving. You were so nice to me, I figured..."

"Don't figure!" I jump off the bed before he tries to kiss me or something.

Snatching my bag off the chair, I quickly pull on my boots and head for the door.

"Where are you going?"

"A walk. I need to walk."

"Do you want me to come with you?"

I can't help shooting him an incredulous glare. For one of the smartest students at Nelson High, he can be pretty stupid.

"What if you get lost?" he murmurs.

"I have GPS on my phone." I tear out of the room and race down the stairs before he can chase me.

I probably shouldn't have left him alone in my room, but I guess it's not really my room, anyway. Skipping down the stairs, I power-walk past the Carmichaels' place. I have no idea where I'm going. I just need to be out. Away.

Maybe I should go home, as in Auckland, New Zealand.

Mom's been bugging me to make it back for Christmas. She's been selling the kiwi summer sun and our annual trip to Pauanui Beach. I could ring in the New Year gazing up at the stars with my toes buried in the sand.

But I don't want to.

Anna's family holidays at the same beach. What if I bump into her? What if all our friends are with her?

Crossing my arms, I hunch over myself, wishing I'd grabbed a jacket. The cool wind whips my hair, but I press forward, walking aimlessly through Nelson until the icy cold gets the better of me and I'm forced into the next restaurant I pass.

The waitress smiles at me, leading me to a booth near the window. I point at the one by the wall and she nods, agreeing to let me have the privacy I'm craving. Before finding Eloise on my bed, I would have wanted to sit front and center...all eyes on me, please.

Not anymore.

Sliding into the booth, I take the menu and then scan the empty eatery. The food must be totally crap because I'm the only person here. I check my watch—ten o'clock. I guess it's not really breakfast or lunchtime, but still.

Clearing my throat, I open the menu and start thumbing through it.

My nose wrinkles as I assess the glossy images. Yeah, I'm totally right. The food here is going to taste disgusting.

The waitress returns and I order a coffee.

"Nothing to eat?"

"No, just the coffee, thanks."

She grins at me, obviously noticing my accent. I look down, silently begging her not to pursue some kind of conversation. Mercifully, she walks away. I follow the line of her white sneakers, tracking their path until I'm brought up short by a large pair of olive-green Vans. My breath hitches as my eyes travel up those jean-clad legs, over the navy and cream letterman jacket before coming face-to-face with the most beautiful eyes I've ever encountered.

Damn those eyes.

I want to hate them.

But I can't, because they belong to Mack.

17

ONE TOUCH CAN CHANGE EVERYTHING

MACK

KAIJA'S EYES fill with tears, and I feel like shit all over again. Rushing to the booth, I slide into the seat opposite her, placing my hands on the table.

"I'm sorry," I murmur.

She dips her chin, her long, silky locks hiding her face from me. "Please, Mack, just leave me alone."

"Not while you're crying. I'm not going anywhere."

With a loud sniff, she swipes at her tears and sits up, staring at me with the same brave face Layla often wears. I see straight through it. Tipping my head with a skeptical frown, I tell her so without saying anything.

She sighs, her expression bunching as she fights more

tears. "Have you no mercy? It's the weekend. No one's here to laugh at the joke you're about to make at my expense."

"Oh, come on. You know it wasn't about that. We were pranking each other. Yes, it may have been a really bizarre way of flirting, but you were into it…until yesterday."

I try to read her expression, but she goes blank on me, giving me nothing. Her eyes dart to the pictures on the wall, cartoon depictions of famous musicians from the fifties and sixties. I glance at the pencil sketches before turning back to study her. The smooth lines of her long face are taut and unrelenting while her neck muscles strain.

She's fighting the urge to look at me.

I settle in and keep staring, unwilling to lose this standoff.

The stubborn beauty makes me wait it out until I eventually sigh and shift in my seat. "I was going to offer you a truce yesterday. You know, after you laughed and called me an asshole for scaring you." I scratch the back of my neck, hopefully looking sheepish and remorseful. "That's what I'd been expecting, anyway. Why'd you freak out so bad?"

She clenches her jaw, her eyes still on the wall. "I can't do this anymore. You won, okay?"

"So, you'll go out with me?" I grin.

Her eyes snap to mine. Wow. Even the frown wrinkling her face is pretty.

I snicker. "That'd be a win for me."

Her fingers quiver as she rubs her forehead. "I meant I'm thinking of going home early. So, you know, you've won. I'm out of your school."

"What?" I jerk in my seat. "No, I don't want that. I...I don't want that at all. I've been trying to get to know you better, not chase you away."

Her flaring nostrils and the way she's bunching her chin tells me that she knows this already.

"Why won't you let me in?" I reach for her hand, but she snatches it back, shuffling out of the booth and grabbing her bag. "Wait." I grab her wrist before she can disappear again.

The move freezes both of us. We stare at each other for a minute and then her eyes slowly track down to my fingers wrapped around her slender wrist. I rub my thumb over her pulse, loving the softness of her skin.

"You can't leave," I whisper. "Please stay. I want you to stay."

Her eyes glass over, turning them a vibrant green, like new leaves in the springtime. Wriggling her wrist free, she tucks her hand into her sweater pocket and runs out the door.

I should chase her, but I'll probably end up pushing her even further away.

Slumping back with a huff, I tap my nail on the hard table before running my thumb over the pads of my fingers. I touched her and, just as I expected, it changed everything.

From the first time I saw Kaija Bennett, I wanted her.

And now I feel like I need her.

18

DETERMINATION DISINTEGRATION

KAIJA

I DON'T KNOW what's going on with me right now. How is it possible that Anderson's touch creeped me out whereas Mack's ignited something within me—a hot, burning addiction I can't stop thinking about. I wanted to stay in that deserted restaurant with Mack's hand around my wrist, his soft hold making me feel more secure than I have since finding Eloise on my bed...or even since the day Eloise left me to go overseas.

But I can't go there.

Mack is too much like Hanson, and that guy brought out the worst in me.

But the look on Mack's face when he pleaded with me

to stay... I never once saw that look on Hanson's face. There's a sweetness and depth to Mack that I want to discover.

I rub my head with a frustrated huff.

On Sunday, I forced myself to hang out with the Fosters. We went for a hike—it was beautiful, the view breathtaking—and all I could think about was Mack.

Anderson didn't say anything about trying to get a little cozy in my bedroom, and I was happy never to mention it again. Spending another six weeks with them was going to be torture if he tried to make another move.

Friends—yes. Something more—no offense, but I can't stomach it. As much as I want Anderson to be one of my new people, he isn't. My heart doesn't triple-thump when I'm around him, I don't feel that buzz or urge to be with him...ever. There's only one person who has that effect on me.

A smile toys with my lips as I walk through the double doors and into the fluorescent-lit hallway of Nelson High. Looks like I'm staying a little longer than I thought.

As much as I want to, I don't seek Mack out. I'm still not sure what I want to say to him or how I want this thing to play out. The war inside me is catastrophic. My natural instincts are tearing my resolve to shreds. Is it simply impossible for me to be someone new? To join a crowd I don't belong in?

I cringe and head for the library. Although I technically don't have to pass any of my classes while I'm here, I don't want to be the only person who hasn't handed in their homework, either. Slumping into a table near the back corner, I pull out my books and slap them down.

"Shhh!" The girl across the table glares at me. I think she's one of Anderson's friends.

I give her a *relax* kind of expression, which only makes her glare harder. Bulging my eyes, I dip my head and get to work. Trying to concentrate is really hard. My mind keeps wandering to Mack.

Mack. Mack. Mack.

Before I know it, I've stopped writing and am running my fingers over the spot on my wrist where his thumb gently caressed me.

This is insane!

I'm not this kind of girl. I don't go gooey. How can one touch turn me into this sappy, lovesick mess?

When we were kids, Eloise and I used to dream about meeting these hot guys. It'd only take one look from them to fall madly in love with us and we'd live happily ever after. I quickly figured out that dreams like that don't come true. So why is it happening to me now, especially when I least deserve it?

"You keep rubbing circles on your wrist like that and you're going to leave a permanent mark."

I glance up, already fighting a smile. Mack's standing there with a knowing grin...a proud, cocky grin. I tuck my wrist beneath the table. I have no defense. He totally caught me daydreaming about his touch on my skin. He knows it. I know it. So all I can say is, "What are you doing in a library?"

Mack takes a seat beside me. "I'll have you—"

"Shhh!" Miss Grump-a-lot glares at me again.

Mack's smile is charming and sweet. "Sorry about that."

Her expression softens, a light blush touching her skin. I roll my eyes and give him a dry frown. He winks at me, his soft, deep chuckle kissing the edge of my face. "I'll have you know," he whispers, "that I happen to love this library."

"Oh, really? Does the quiet solitude do it for you?"

"No." He tips his head towards the rows of books behind us. "There's a great make-out spot in the back corner."

A smile wipes out my frown and I only just catch the

laughter wanting to break free. I bite my lips together and shake my head at him. "You're beyond help, you know that?"

"Yeah, I've known that for years, so I just go ahead and embrace it."

I poke my tongue into my cheek, trying to ward off the next flashy grin. I don't want to encourage him.

But, oh man, I do!

"So, you stayed." Mack's playful charm disappears behind that sweet softness I spotted on Saturday. His dark eyes drink me in, telling me I'm beautiful.

I swallow and try to look away. But I can't. My brain is saying one thing but my body's doing another. I gaze at his gorgeous face. It's like being soaked in the warm sun on a cold winter's day.

"Meet me after school," he whispers.

"I can't." My response is automatic. I don't mean it, but fear is making my resolve thick and strong.

"Yes, you can." He leans closer. His brown eyes are so dark and intense, like dark cocoa with a hint of chili— my favorite treat. "There's something between us, Kaija. I don't know why you're trying so hard to deny it."

My secret rears its ugly head, choking me. I can't swallow past the boulder lodged in my throat.

The corner of Mack's mouth twitches, then rises into a half-smile. He rests his elbow on the table, angling his body so all I can see is him. All I can sense is his strength and masculinity—his powerful thighs stretching towards me, his strong arms ready to catch me if I try to bolt. Is it bad that I want them to?

It should be bad!

But I want him to. I want him to catch me and never let go.

Maybe he can make me forget…or pretend that I never did what I did.

"Thing is…" The tips of his fingers graze down my cheekbone. The delicacy of his touch contradicts the raging impact it has on me—so soft, yet so strong. "I'm used to getting what I want, Kaija. It's always come so easy, but you… You've made me work for it." He grins. "And I've never wanted anything more."

I lean away from him, my eyebrows dipping together— one final attempt to capture my resolve. "I'm not some-thing you can just have."

"It's not like…" He closes his eyes and cringes. "I'm explaining myself really badly. You…" He glances at study girl, then shoots out of his chair, gently taking my wrist and pulling me into one of the fiction rows. We stop in front of a line of Harry Potter books and I let him box me in. "I like you. More than I've ever liked anybody. You see through my bullshit and you aren't afraid to call me on it. I need you in my life."

"You *need* me." His words are doing a number on my insides, but I have to at least scoff at his dramatic statement.

"Yes, I need you." His hand is on my face again, cupping my cheek and drawing me in like a moth to a flame. "Because when I'm not with you, I'm thinking about you. Like, all the time. It's kind of consuming and it's making me a little crazy." I'm transfixed by his eyes. They hold me steady. "I want to spend time with you. I want to figure out this power you have over me."

"You're making me sound like a witch," I whisper. It's a breathy, pathetic sound that I only just manage to squeak out.

"Come on." He flashes me the megawatt version of his charming smile, and I'm embarrassed to admit that it completely owns me. "Look me in the eye and tell me you don't feel something too."

I don't have to force myself to do what he asks.

The only response I have left is to smile and admit, "Okay, so maybe I can't deny it anymore."

His face takes on a triumphant glow. Not the arrogant, cocky one, but the thrilled-to-be-in-this-position one. I've just made his freaking day. And he's about to make mine. The smile slips from his lips, his gaze searching mine. I silently give him permission and he leans towards me. His warm breath skims my skin, accelerating my heart rate and—

"You two better be searching for something to read." A sharp voice jolts us apart. With wide eyes, I turn to take in the librarian. She's a short, rotund woman with a merry—well, usually merry—smile. Right now, she doesn't look so impressed. Her fist is perched on her hip while her eyes flash us a warning.

At exactly the same time, Mack and I let out these sheepish, breathy chuckles that do nothing to hide our intent.

"Get to class."

She tips her thumb at the door and we shuffle past her. Mack's behind me as I start gathering up my books and shoving them into my bag. His hand rests lightly on my lower back when he whispers into my ear. "Meet me on the field after school."

And with that, he disappears. So, I'm left with a stomach full of manic butterflies and a resolve that's no bigger than a dried-up raisin.

19

THE TRUTH FAUCET

MACK

ROXY'S LEANING against my locker at the end of the school day. Usually, this makes a slow smile creep across my face. A little flirt with Roxy is always fun, but not today. Not when I'm due to meet the most delectable kiwi girl in just a few minutes.

"Hey, Rox. What's shakin'?"

Her smile is stunning. It always has been...and she knows it.

I clear my throat and tip my head to the side, a subtle way of telling her to move off my locker. She picks up the hint and steps into my space.

"So, I was thinking." Her hand lands on my chest, then

glides up until she's playing with the collar of my jacket.

"Oh yeah?" I try to keep my voice low and distant.

"The season's over and it's getting too cold for the bonfires. I kind of miss it. Don't you?"

I work my jaw to the side. "Yeah, the end of the season always sucks."

She simpers. Her bright eyes, usually so alluring, have nothing on Kaija's emeralds. A smile twitches my lips. Roxy misinterprets it, pressing her body against mine. "It doesn't have to, you know. I'm sure you and I could find an excuse to celebrate something." Her lips brush my cheek. "Why don't we go somewhere?"

I step away from her with a knowing smile. "I don't think so."

"What?" The sharp frown wrinkling her forehead makes her look like a cartoon character.

I run my hand down her arm, trying to soften her glare. Roxy's one of those girls the word 'vengeance' was invented for. I'm not about to cross her…but I won't be putting Kaija in the line of fire, either. So I shrug and tell her a big, fat one. "I'm not free today." I don't really want to say it, but I tack on, "Maybe some other time."

My brush-off goes over okay and she glides past me with a "You can count on it."

I clench my jaw as her fingers trail across my back. Glancing to my right, I notice a few sets of eyes on me. They all turn away as I scan the rest of the hallway. It's like crabs scuttling back into their holes in the sand. I fling my locker open and quickly rearrange the books I need. The sharp bang of my locker closing echoes down the hallway. Hitching my bag onto my shoulder, I turn to head for the field and notice Finn, Colt and Tori heading toward me. I spin on my heel, pick up my pace and duck out of view, going the long way around to get to my date.

I don't know why I feel the need to hide it. Maybe I don't want them tagging along or ruining this for me.

I don't want anything to ruin it, which is why the second my Vans hit the grass, I run across to my love-at-first-sight and start talking. "Sorry I'm late. Roxanne Carmichael tried to make a pass at me and I brushed her off, although to soften the blow, I kind of gave her the impression that I might be interested. But I'm actually not. She's just not the kind of girl you want to cross."

By the time I stop, Kaija is giving me one of her bust-my-heart-wide-open smiles. "Hi to you too."

I cringe. "Sorry, I just thought you should know. Roxy and I have…" I hiss. "Well, it's… We kind of sometimes get together and then we… It's never serious.

Just making out, really, but I'm not interested in that anymore and—"

"You can stop talking now." She shoves my shoulder and laughs. "I get it. I know the type. You don't have to explain anything to me."

"But I want to. I don't want anything to come between us."

Her face flickers with a frown and I start to worry that I'm coming on too strong. Of course I am! I'm a lovesick weirdo who's never felt this way before. As much as I hate it, I crave it. This giddy, light-headed thing is a trip. I barely know this girl and she makes me want to be a better version of myself. Other than my dad, no one's ever stirred that kind of motivation in me.

I bite my lips together and rub the back of my neck before I'm tempted to say all that out loud.

"So…" Kaija spreads her hands wide and does a slow spin. "Is this your place of worship?"

I snicker and gaze across the vibrant, green grass, the clean-cut white lines, the field that's absorbed my sweat, my blood—my soul—for the last four years. It's strange how nostalgic I feel. I haven't even left yet but the idea of never running onto this field with a Raiders uniform on again makes me feel a combination of sadness and relief.

Kaija's long locks fall over her shoulder as she tips her head to study me. Her green eyes tighten at the corners. "Wow, I've seen that look before."

"What look?" My eyes round slightly, my hands diving into my jacket pockets.

"Usually when you talk sports with the captain of a team, they start going on about how amazing it is and how they can't wait to take it further. But you…" She points at me. "You look like you could walk away at any second."

How the hell did she see that?

I swallow and shake my head. "No, I'm excited. I mean, I'm supposed to be signing with the Boise State Broncos. In February, I'll give them my letter of intent, and then I'll go on to follow in my father's footsteps."

"He pressuring you into it?" Kaija crosses her arms, her keen eyes sparking.

"Uh…no. He's, um… He's dead." My jaw works to the side and I have to glance into the empty stands to hide the emotion tearing through me. Even after all this time, it still hurts to say it.

Kaija rushes over to me and touches my arm, her long fingers gliding down to my elbow. "I'm so sorry."

That's what everyone says, but somehow from her, it's a comfort. It gives me the courage to look into her eyes.

They're swimming with a heartfelt compassion that pulls the truth right out of my mouth.

"He died of cancer when I was in middle school. I threw everything into the game. It was the only way I could deal with it. Playing made me feel closer to him, but I don't know…" I sigh, fisting the side of my hair. "I just… I don't know if I want to make it my life, you know? Everyone expects it, though. If I don't sign…" I shake my head with a sharp huff, picturing my mother's crushed expression and my team's confusion.

This is so not going the way I'd spent most of my day imagining. I wanted to have some fun with this girl, not expose my soul. I haven't voiced this shit to anyone, because there's nothing I can do about it.

Kaija's gaze penetrates my shield, burning a hole right through to my core. Her wide lips form a sweet smile that I want to etch into my memory. "My eldest brother, Mitchell, was one of those naturally talented athletes, just like you. My dad has been involved with rugby his whole life. He coached for years and is now the sports director of a private school in Auckland. Anyway, he was super keen for Mitch to take it all the way. I think he could have been an All Black if he'd really wanted to, but…he didn't." Her eyebrows rise as she obviously relives a memory. "When he told Dad he was giving up the game to focus on his studies, I've never heard our house so quiet. Everyone sat around that table totally shell-shocked." She chuckles. "Dad came around eventually, and Mitch is close to graduating with a degree in medicine. He wants to be a sports doctor."

Something in my chest unravels as I listen to her.

"I can't imagine what he went through finding the courage to tell Dad the truth. Thankfully, parents love their kids... Well, most parents do, and they want their kids to be happy. I know your father's not with you anymore, but even beyond the grave, he'd want you to be happy, right?"

"I wish I could ask him." My voice is husky and raw.

"You don't need to." Kaija squeezes my elbow. "I'm telling ya, mate. He wants you to be happy."

I grin at her words. "You seem pretty sure about that."

"If you played to feel close to him, you must have loved him...and kids only love their parents that much when their parents have loved them like they should. Your dad must have been an amazing man."

"Yeah, he was," I murmur, struggling to swallow the lump in my throat.

With another melt-my-heart grin, Kaija wraps her arms around me, resting her head on my shoulder and giving me a tight squeeze. "It's going to be okay, Mack. You'll find your way."

I hug her back, fighting a burning in my eyes. I don't know what it's all about, but like hell I'm crying in front of this girl. Kissing the top of her head, I run my arms down her back and then lean away from her.

"This is not at all how I expected this date to go."

"It's a date?" Kaija's eyes dance with mischief. "Sheesh, you sure know how to impress a girl. Here I was thinking you'd be putting on airs, and you just go straight for the gut-wrenching truth."

"Hey, that's completely your fault." I let her go and point at her.

"Me? All I did was stand here, and you just opened up like a burst pipe!"

"It's not my fault you're a truth faucet. I haven't told anyone any of this stuff and you give me one smile and I'm torn wide open."

She laughs. "It's called a tap, not a faucet."

I snatch her wrist and pull her to my side, loving her height and the way she fits against me. "Hey, you're in my turf now; it's called a faucet."

"Okay, I'll let you have that one." She steps back and looks down between us. "So, what turf am I standing on at this moment?"

I look down, scanning the straight white lines painted on the field. "We're in the red zone right now."

"The red zone. That sounds dangerous."

I love the playful glint in her eyes.

"Well, it can be. You see…" I pull her against me… again. I can't help it. "This is the space just before the end zone. You want to make sure your opposition stays well clear of your red zone."

"I see." She glides her hands up my arms, linking her fingers behind my neck. "And what about a foreign girl with an adorable accent?"

"Oh, her?" I tip my head, fighting a smile. "Well, if I ever find one, I'll be telling her she can hang out in my red zone anytime."

"Oh!" She slaps my chest, jerking out of my arms with a laugh. "You are so not getting kissed this afternoon."

"Come on, that was a joke."

"You were so close too." She puts on a pout. "Such a shame."

I point at her. "I'm getting that kiss."

"Nah, mate, you're really not." But the sparkle in her eyes says otherwise.

A low growl reverberates in my chest. She lets out a

scream and starts sprinting down the field, her melodic laughter spurring me on.

I chase after her. She's faster than I thought she'd be and really makes me work for it, but I catch her in the opposite red zone. Wrapping my arms around her stomach, I lift her off the ground and swing her around until her legs become propellers. Her long hair tickles my neck. Her laughter surrounds me. She's taking over every one of my senses, and I can't remember the last time I felt this light and happy. I don't even need to kiss her. When it comes to this girl, just hanging out is enough.

20

A RICKETY MESS

KAIJA

MACK SWINGS me around until we both tumble to the ground, dizzy wrecks. Shifting up my body, he nestles himself against me, gazing into my eyes and gently brushing wisps of hair off my face. It feels magical.

I've kissed plenty of guys before but never experienced this kind of anticipation. His lips are so close. My mouth is buzzing as he inches towards me.

And then his phone rings.

I flinch while he groans and presses his forehead against mine. Reaching into his back pocket, he yanks his phone free. The way his face flickers with worry when he reads the screen makes me curious. We sit up together as he answers the call.

"Hey, sis. What's up?" His bright tone is forced; I can tell by the tension in his jaw. "You did what?" He closes his eyes, scrubbing a hand down his face and suddenly looking twice his age.

I skim his arm with my fingers. He flashes me a pained look of apology, then mutters, "Yeah, okay. I'll come get ya."

Sliding the phone back into his pocket, he stands tall and reaches down to help me up.

"Everything okay?" I brush my butt. Keeping the disappointment from my voice is kind of impossible so I just lower my tone instead.

"Yeah, just my…" He sighs, scraping his fingers through his hair. "My sister is…" His full lips purse, and agitation radiates off him.

I smile and reach for his hand. "You're a good brother."

He threads his fingers between mine, then looks at our connection while he's speaking. "I feel like her father sometimes and I really hate it. She skipped out of school this afternoon to go shopping with Michelle and they just happened to get busted by Principal Matthis. She's in detention now and he's threatening to call Mom. I need to go smooth things over. She and Mom haven't been the same since our stepfather came along."

My heart pinches tight, sensing there's more to the story. "Like I said, you're a good brother."

His thumb rubs over mine. Such a simple gesture, yet it feels so amazing.

"What the hell is she going to do next year when I'm in Boise?"

"She's going to be okay, Mack. She has to learn to fight her own battles eventually, right?"

"Yeah, I guess." He sighs. "At least I can still come home on the weekends."

"She'll figure it out. Sometimes life dishes out wake-up calls you can't ignore." My throat swells, making it hard to swallow. I suddenly feel undeserving of his touch, so I wriggle my hand free and tuck it into my back pocket. "I'll let you get going."

I turn to leave but he captures my hand before I can escape. I let him pull me back to his side. "I need your number. I want to call you tonight and see if I can convince you to kiss me tomorrow."

I grin and have to seriously fight the laughter bubbling in my chest. Stepping back, I hold out my hand. "Gimme your phone."

He passes it over and I memorize that sexy little smirk of his.

I tap in my US number and hand it back with a grin. "Good luck playing dad."

He rolls his eyes and lets out another groan before squeezing the phone in his hand and jogging back into school. I watch him until he's out of sight.

Falling in love with Mack Mahoney is going to be a piece of cake.

I should be terrified, but I can't stop buzzing. I walk back to the Fosters' with a bounce in my step. I eat dinner, fighting a smile the whole time. I've never behaved this way before. Guys don't make me gooey…

I guess I just hadn't met the right one yet.

At eight o'clock, my phone starts beeping with a Face-Time call. I snatch it off my desk and head for the bed, flopping onto my pillow and answering with a smile.

"G'day."

"I don't think I'll ever be able to get enough of that accent." Mack winks at me and my heart melts. Seriously, what am I turning into?

I roll onto my stomach, perching my chin on my hand and smiling down at the screen. "How'd it go?"

"Oh, you know, the usual. Principal Matthis likes me, so I used my charm to save my sister's butt, promising him that it won't happen again. I drove her home, swearing to keep her antics on the down-low." He rolls his eyes. "Sometimes I wonder if I should just out her to Mom, but I don't think our house is built to withstand a nuclear meltdown."

I laugh. "Thank God college is just around the corner, right?"

"Hmmmm." He looks sad but tries to hide it behind a cocky smile. "So, rugby. You guys have a red zone in that sport?"

"Nice topic change. Very subtle."

He winces. "Please, just let me have it."

The silent plea for mercy sweeping across his face does me in, so I give in with a short nod. I start telling him all about the sport that has dominated my home since before I can remember.

Four hours later, we end the call. I've moved from my stomach to my side, to lying on my back with my feet resting on the wall. My legs flop down to the mattress and I curl onto my side. I feel like a rickety mess. Brushing a thumb over my phone screen, I let out a soft squeal and hug it to my chest, already looking forward to a repeat. My brain tries to dump all over my happy parade with a reminder that I've spent most of our four-hour chat steering the conversation away from my high school experience. Mack was nice enough not to notice. At least I don't think he did. We talked rugby, football, family, movies, music, cars, football again, touched on rugby one last time, and then spent half an hour saying goodbye to each other.

I nearly said, "No, you hang up," but caught myself in the nick of time. I am so not going to be that pathetic, needy girl. Yet, when it comes to Mack I want more… and maybe a little more, and then a pinch more after that.

I close my eyes with a dreamy smile. Inching up the bed, I snuggle into my pillow, not even bothering to change into my jim-jams before falling asleep.

———

So, I get my rinse and repeat on the FaceTime call. Mack calls me each night at eight and we talk until midnight. You'd think we'd run out of things to say, but we don't. Childhood stories and memories of his dad take up a lot of time. Not that I'm complaining. I love listening to him, watching his face as he opens up about stuff he must have never told anyone. I feel so privileged that he's willing to open up to me…and then I feel insanely guilty for not telling him the truth about my life.

But I can't.

It'll change everything between us. I'm scared he'll never look at me the same way again. I don't want that brilliant gaze of his to change. I want him to keep thinking I'm this amazing, love-worthy person.

Spinning the ball in my hands, I walk up the school steps and head to Mack's locker. Most of me feels that light, happy giddiness I've enjoyed all week. And then there's the small, constant guilt-bug inside, chowing on my stomach lining. Lifting my chin, I pull my shoulders back and ignore it. It's Friday, and the first afternoon Mack has been free since our non-kiss date on the football field. We still haven't had a chance to make out, and I'm hoping to change that this afternoon.

Mack's standing at his locker, chatting with Layla and Roxy. The blue-eyed brunette is playing with her hair and doing the hip-jut thing. I roll my eyes and wait her out.

Although Mack and I have both acknowledged we more than like each other, we don't really want to make it public. I can't even explain why. We both seem protective of whatever we've got going on, and exposing it will put us in the line of fire. I don't want to dwell on it, but we're on limited time as it is. We want to suck every sweet moment we can from this, and that's not going to happen surrounded by his posse of coolness.

Mack nods, focusing on Layla, but then Roxy starts talking and his gaze wanders the hallway. He spots me hovering around the corner. Our eyes connect and he fights a smile. I grin, sticking out my hip and doing the ultimate hair toss. Okay, now he's fighting laughter. His face is getting red trying to contain it. I wriggle my eyebrows and wink at him.

Wiping his mouth, he coughs over his laugh and then checks his watch. I can't hear what he's saying, but thirty seconds later he's loping down the hallway towards me. With a triumphant smirk, I position myself in a quiet alcove next to a janitor's closet. Mack appears, his gorgeous face and towering persona sending electric sparks right through my center.

"G'day, Kiwi Girl."

I snicker as he attempts my accent. "Don't even try. You'll never pull it off."

"I'm going to keep working on it anyway." He leans closer and gives me a sexy wink. "Nice to see you in the flesh, pretty lady. Am I going to get my kiss this afternoon?"

"It's highly possible." I pull away from him when a group of girls rushes past us. Thankfully, they're all so busy jabbering that they don't even notice me. Lifting the ball in my hands, I pass it to him.

"Is that a…?"

"Rugby ball, yes. I thought maybe I could teach you how to play."

His eyes light up like I've just given him a million dollars. "That's going to be like the sexiest thing ever."

A loud laugh bursts out of me. "Hardly! But it should be heaps of fun."

His grin tells me I've said something very un-American. He doesn't say anything, just leans forward so his lips brush my cheek on the way to my ear. "I'm looking forward to it, Kiwi Girl. See you in the red zone."

"I'll be there."

The bell jolts us apart. I soak in his luscious wink, then check out his butt as he saunters away from me. He is all kinds of good-looking.

"Mhm." I lick my bottom lip and watch until he's out of sight.

Spinning for my locker, I race to change my books before I'm late for class. I still can't believe I'm acting like such a lovesick fool. Of all the crushes I've had in my lifetime, I've never experienced anything like this. I wouldn't even put it in the crush zone—this is something else entirely.

I never expected this to happen when I came here. I seriously don't deserve it. But my heart is ruling this one, and I don't think my head will ever be loud enough to outshout whatever the heck is going on inside of me.

At least that's what I convince myself...until I turn up to my study period and find a very serious-faced Anderson Foster waiting for me in the library.

21

MY GIRL

MACK

I STAND on the field waiting for my girl. Can I call her that? It feels right. I've never wanted to call anyone else that before. A smile tugs at the edge of my mouth. Kiwi Girl has definitely done a number on me. I'm loving it.

Spinning the rugby ball in my hands, I catch it and rub my thumb over the bumpy surface. It's a slightly different shape to the football I've spent my life holding, but I kind of like it. I raise my arm above my head, faking a spiral pass down the field, but the ball's bigger and seems to be telling me not to throw it that way... I'm doing it all wrong.

I fumble the ball and catch it just before it hits the ground, tossing it up then leaping forward to catch it against my chest. Since meeting Kaija, I've watched a few rugby games on YouTube. I kind of understand the game. Kaija talked me through the rules, and seeing them in action helped me get a better handle on them. I have a pretty good grasp of the overall concept now, anyway. I watched the 2015 World Cup final where the All Blacks won. From what I could gather, it was a really exciting game. I liked the fast pace and flow, and some of the tackles were epic. Seeing the guys dive across the line when they scored their tries was awesome. And just quietly, I loved that warrior dance thing they do before the game. It's fierce, man. I hope I can get to a live game someday.

The thought of going with Kaija makes me buzz, then deflate. Reality pinches at the back of my mind. She's going to be leaving soon, flying half a world away. I don't know how we're going to do it. Will she even be into a long-distance relationship? Could I handle one? I shove the question from my mind, not wanting it to shit all over our rugby date. All I can do right now is cherish every second I have with her. We can deal with the rest later.

I catch a movement out of the corner of my eye and spin towards it. Kaija is shuffling across the grass, her arms crossed and her expression dark and forlorn. My gut pitches, the warning traveling through me so fast I feel light-headed. Dropping the ball, I run towards her, resting my hands on her shoulders and bending down to look at her glistening eyes.

"What's the matter?"

She shrugs me off, turning away from my grasp with a gentle sniff. "I think that maybe this is a bad idea."

My twisted insides wrench and writhe. I clench my jaw against the verbal attack that wants to bust out of me. I hate how quick the anger flashes, but when people blow me off without an explanation it riles me big time.

Kaija can be a little hedgy. I've let it slide because it hasn't affected our time together, but if she's going to brush me off, especially after the week we've just had together, then she's got some explaining to do.

Smashing my teeth together, I will the steam to evaporate and force out what I hope will be a light joke. "What, you don't think I can learn a real man's game?"

She doesn't buy it. Instead, she spins to face me with a green gaze that threatens to rip me in half. "I can't hang out with you anymore, Mack. It's..." She huffs, her fingers pinching into her jacket. "People don't like it."

"Who cares what people think!" I don't mean to shout the words, but it's a nice release and so I go for it, even throwing my arms wide.

My harsh tone doesn't rattle her. Instead, she runs her

fingers through her hair and murmurs, "I'm only here for a few more weeks. It's seriously not worth—"

"What are you doing?" I have to interrupt her. I can't hear any kind of *break up* words come out of her.

"I'm being realistic." She shrugs, her gaze glued to the grass beneath us.

I step into her space, so close she's forced to look up at me. Her eyes flash wide for a second and she tries to turn away, but I gently pinch her chin, forcing her to face me. "No, you're acting scared. What happened to you between this morning and right now?"

Her eyebrows bunch as she snaps her eyes shut and tries to avoid me.

"Did someone say something to you?" My insides are going nuts. It's kind of hard to keep my voice calm when all I feel like doing is smashing the person who put that look on her face.

Her lips press into a thin line before she steps back with another huff. "Maybe. I… He's right, though! I shouldn't be hanging out with guys like you. I should stick with my people."

"That's horse shit! You are my people."

She slaps her hand over her eyes and squeezes her temples. "Not according to Anderson Foster!"

Anger spurts hot and fast through my core. I'm going to strangle that noxious weed.

"You're seriously going to let that brainiac get to you? That guy couldn't be more boring if he tried. And he's saying you fit better with him than me? I thought he was supposed to be intelligent, not a dipshit!"

"Don't talk about him like that." She scrapes her fingers through her hair, bunching it at the nape of her neck.

"What? He's trying to pull us apart and you're standing up for him?" I can't control my tone right now. I don't want to yell at this beautiful girl, but I'm damn riled. "What the hell do you really want, Kaija? Because I thought it was me."

"I can't want you, Mack!" Her entire body goes taut as she shouts at me, her wild eyes flashing with desperation before she whispers, "You don't get it."

The expression on her face kills my anger. A shockwave of protectiveness fires through me and I step into her space again, wrapping my arms around her tense body and resting my chin on her shoulder. Rubbing slow circles on her back, I softly ask, "What did he say to you?"

Her voice is muffled against my shirt, but I still hear every word. "He just reminded me that I'm only here for a short time and I need to be careful...and he's right." She pushes her fists into my chest and as much as I want to tighten my hold, I force myself to let her go. "We shouldn't…" She shakes her head.

"Yes, we should." Before I can think better of it, I cup her face and dive for her lips. It's not exactly how I pictured our first kiss, but I need her to know how I feel. And since my words aren't working…

Her lips are soft, warm and luscious, like I knew they would be. I press my mouth against them, then swipe my tongue along her bottom lip. There's nothing sweet and delicate about this kiss; it's rough and passionate. I pour everything I have into it. Threading my fingers through her hair, I hold her close, willing her to give into the pulsing chemistry between us…and she does. With a soft whimper, she meets my tongue with an urgency that gives away her desire. Our tongues lash together like they can't get enough of the heat.

I'm waiting for her arms to wrap around me, for her fingers to entwine behind my neck. If they do, I'm picking her up. I want her legs around my waist. I want to hold her so close that nothing can come between us.

But her arms don't move, at least not the way I want them to.

She lets out a cry and pushes me off her. "This can never happen." Her breath hitches and she covers her lips with the back of her hand, shaking her head and spinning away from me. She's about to break into a run, but I lurch forward and catch her before she can. Wrapping my arms around her, I rest my chin in the crook of her neck and press my lips against her jawline. I expect her to struggle and kick. Her back is pressed against my torso and I'm holding her pretty tight, ready to battle it out, but she just kind of sags against me, her stomach jerking as she fights a sob.

Rubbing my nose against her cheek, I will my voice not to shake as I whisper, "We're meant to be together. I've known it since the second I saw you. I know it because I've been acting crazy trying to win you over."

She turns towards my voice and I kiss her cheek.

"But you don't know me." She sounds so broken. So scared.

An uneasy disquiet stirs within as I gently spin her so I can look into those eyes. They're shimmering and vibrant, tugging at my soul like nothing I've known. I brush her tears away with the back of my finger. "I've talked more to you in one week than I have to anyone my entire life."

"You don't know what I've done." Her expression crumples. "I'm no good for you, Mack. We'll just bring out the worst in each other."

"What are you hiding?" My voice trembles. The emotions in me are so thick and strong I don't know what to do with them. "Why are you fighting something you know is right?"

She flicks my hand off her face. "Because you wouldn't feel this way if you knew what a horrible, arrogant bitch I am."

"What are you talking about?" I hate hearing those words come out of her mouth. No one talks about my girl that way, not even her.

"I nearly got someone killed! Do you honestly want to be with someone like that?"

The words act like an air vacuum, sucking the life out of the empty stadium. We both stand there frozen for a second, jolted by her raw honesty. Her eyes round, fear skittering across her face as she stumbles away from me. Her foot catches on the bag she dumped somewhere during our argument and she starts to fall.

I rush to catch her, gripping her arm and hauling her back against me. She crashes into my chest and I gather her in my arms, sweeping up her legs before lowering us to the ground. My legs cross and I nestle her into my lap, then press my lips to her forehead, kneading the back of her neck as she starts to cry. Her heart-wrenching sobs remind me of Layla at Dad's grave when his coffin was lowered into the ground.

My protective instincts had been working on overdrive then and they're doing the same now. I want to wipe away her pain. Hell, I'll take it as my own if I have to. Hearing the hitch in her breath followed by those soft little whimpers, feeling her damp cheeks as she lets the tears fall unchecked… It's enough to crush any guy. I encase her in my arms, cradling her against me until the sobs ebb to quiet sniffles.

"Talk to me," I whisper. "Tell me the truth."

"You'll never look at me the same," she murmurs, curling her fingers into my jacket.

I gaze up at the blue sky above us, so crystal clear. The grass beneath us is cold and will soon be making my muscles ache, but I'm not moving. Not until she tells me everything. Running my fingers down the back of her hair, I kiss the side of her head and promise, "Whatever you say is not going to change how I feel about you."

She pulls away from me, gazing into my eyes with a look of agony. "It should."

"Let me be the judge of that." I smile at her, caressing her tear-stained cheek with the tips of my fingers. "Trust me. Let me be your truth faucet."

A fleeting grin crests her lips before she closes her eyes with a heavy sigh.

"When I was a kid, my best friend was Eloise Cochran. We did everything together. But then just before high school, she moved to Myanmar with her parents. I was kind of heartbroken and I guess a little bitter, not that it was her fault. I just felt sort of lost without her. When I started high school, I became friends with this girl, Anna. She was part of the cool crowd and I fit in way easier than I thought I would. My older brother, Corbin, was one of the hot guys at the school and I think they wanted to get in with me to get with him. You know what they're like." She rolls her eyes. "But once he left, I still had a place with them."

Her surprise makes me grin. She really has no idea how amazing she is.

"Anyway, by the time Eloise returned, I had a bunch of new friends and she was this girl who'd been living in the middle of nowhere. She assumed we'd be instant friends again… Maybe I thought we would too, but… my friends at the time took great delight in teasing her. She was so awkward and out of the loop. Any flaw they could find, and they found heaps, they went after it. Even her last name—Cochran—was turned into various cock jokes. You can imagine all the mileage they got out of that." Her face scrunches, her cheeks burning red while her voice peters out to barely audible. "Rather than helping her, I just… I didn't want to be lumped with her. I was scared of being kicked out of the cool crowd, becoming the butt of their jokes. I was worried I'd become an open target." Her lips tremble as she sucks in a breath. "So, rather than doing the right thing, I turned into them, became this nasty, horrible, taunting, manipulative…"

"Okay, I get it. You were mean." I wave my hand through the air, needing to cut her self-deprecation short.

"I was brutal." Her voice breaks over the word brutal, her face bunching as a fresh wave of tears fills her eyes. "I don't know how she put up with it for as long as she did. She just quietly endured it, stoic and strong. I felt bad sometimes, but most of the time I just brushed it off, thinking she could handle it." Tears course down Kaija's cheeks. I try to wipe them away, but she stops me with a shake of her head, swiping at her own tears.

I can't help wondering if this is the first time she's ever let the whole truth out, because it seems to be almost cathartic for her. The color of her eyes changes, a hint of blue storming into the green as a look of sick regret courses over her face.

"About a month ago, I got home from school and she was lying on my bed, white as a ghost. Red-rimmed eyes, blue lips." Her eyes go wide and glassy, as if she's seeing it all over again.

I swallow, recognizing her expression. I'd seen it before, the day we'd jumped out and scared her in the hallway. "Shit, the masks. I am so sorry."

"You didn't know." She shook her head, trying to smile

at me but failing. "No one can know. I'm so ashamed. She downed a bottle of pills because of me."

The words hurt her and I feel them like a punch in the gut. I want to make it better, to take away her pain, so lamely I choke out, "You don't know that."

"I do!" She squeaks. "She left a note about not being able to do it anymore. School was a battlefield and her armor had disintegrated. She felt naked and alone, pelted and bruised. She just wanted it all to stop." Kaija sniffs, pressing the back of her quivering hand against her lips, then biting the skin.

I gently pull her hand away before she can leave teeth marks. Rubbing my thumb over the tender skin, I stay quiet so she can keep going and let it all out. It's killing me to see her like this, but I have to let her finish.

"She said, 'I'm tired of feeling so afraid and sick all the time. I can't fight anymore. I'm done.'" Kaija's chin trembles as she looks into my eyes. "I pushed her over the edge, Mack, and she made that abundantly clear by trying to finish herself on *my* bed. It was like her closing statement."

"But she didn't die."

"No, I called an ambulance and did CPR, kept her alive until they got there and took over."

I give her a soft smile, my chest squeezing tight. "So, you saved her life."

"Ironic, right? Yet another reason for her to hate me." Her biting words are bitter and hateful. I know all of her emotion is directed inward and I have to stop it.

"You did the right thing."

"Only after I did so many wrong things I lost count. I was a coward, Mack. More worried about my status than someone who needed me." She closes her eyes, a few more tears slipping down her cheek. "After it happened, I told my boyfriend and he turned on me, made me feel like I was totally to blame, and then all my 'friends'…" She makes air quotes while I try to wrestle the word 'boyfriend' out of my brain. I clench my jaw and tell myself her derogatory tone must mean they've broken up. "…joined in, spreading rumors and exaggerating the story. I went into hiding, and when I came here, I swore I wouldn't get involved with those kinds of people again. Girls like Roxy, and guys like… well, you, bring out the worst in me. I don't want to be that horrible person again."

"You think I bring out the worst in you?" I smirk, desperate to lighten the moment.

She fights a smile, shaking her head with a perplexed frown. "That's what I don't get. I've spent most of high school dating guys just like you, but being around *you* makes me feel…like nothing I've ever known. But you're everything I shouldn't want! You're cool and gorgeous. You can prank like a pro. All the guys look up to you, all the girls want to get with you. I can't become like them again, Mack."

"You won't."

"How do you know that?" The question shoots out—sharp and desperate, her internal struggle so obvious.

I lick the edge of my mouth, knowing that answering too fast might come off as callous. I want her to know I believe every word I'm saying. Cupping her cheek, I gaze into those eyes that capture me and rub my thumb across her cheekbone. "Because you've had the living crap scared out of you. I can see it in your eyes. You will *never* go back to being that girl. But denying who you are isn't going to work, either. You can't do that for the rest of your life. You'll turn yourself inside out trying."

"You're one to talk," she mutters, her right eyebrow arching. "You're totally living the lie too."

I snicker, my tone serious when I finally reply. "Yeah, I am." I blink, my eyes skimming the ground before landing back on hers. "So maybe we should do something about that. Maybe all this change starts with us."

A soft smile crests her lips as she places her hand over mine. "Why do you do that?"

"Do what?"

"Say shit that makes me fall even harder for you."

I grin at her dry expression. "I mean it, you know."

She nods and whispers, "That's why I'm falling."

Her words draw me in, pulling me towards her lips. Our second kiss is soft and filled with something I've never experienced—kind of like a promise. And it's in this moment that I'm certain she's *my* girl and I'll be calling her that for a very long time.

22

ADORKABLE

KAIJA

"NO." I laugh. The giggles rupturing my stomach are making it hard to run. "Pass back. Your arm movement is all wrong."

Mack gives me a doubtful frown and tries again, flicking the rugby ball off to the side. He looks awkward, which I find hilarious. The most athletic, gorgeous, coolest guy in school and he can't even throw a rugby ball.

I race for the ball, catching it on the bounce, and press it into my stomach, bending over so I can laugh a little more.

"Give me a break. I'm used to throwing the ball over

my shoulder." He storms towards me, muttering, "Stupid game. You kiwis don't know anything."

I pop up, faking insult, but I can't pull it off. Red-faced, grumpy-ass Mack is kind of cute. I tip my head, putting on my best smile. "You know you're completely a*dork*able when you're trying to play a *real* man's sport, right?"

He stops short, his dry glare making me chuckle. "A*dork*able? You did not just say that to me." He growls and starts running straight at me.

I squeal and throw the ball at him, spinning fast to make a quick escape. He deflects the ball easily and keeps charging, wrapping his arms around me and lifting me up. I yelp and start laughing as he tackles me to the ground, making sure he turns at the last minute so he's the one hitting the grass first.

I run my fingers down his strong jawline and press my thumb into his deep chin dimple. "We need to work on your tackling too." I grin before cutting off his argument with my lips.

He lets out a pleasant moan, like he's tasting chocolate for the first time, and drags his hand up my back. His fingers thread into my hair, cupping the back of my head. I suck his bottom lip into my mouth, hungry for a taste of him. We only shared our first kiss two days ago, but Mack's lips are like a drug. I promised to teach him rugby this weekend and the reason he's probably doing so badly is because we keep getting distracted. But how can we not? His mouth was made for mine.

I shift my knee, tucking it between his legs and nestling myself more firmly against his chest. His strong arms anchor me to him, holding me steady, promising to keep me close. I tip my head, delving deeper into his exquisite mouth. My hair slips over my shoulder, cocooning us from the world. I don't feel the sun's feeble attempt to break through the clouds. I don't feel the cold grass threatening to freeze our limbs. Mack's jacket rustles as he runs his hand down to my hip, splaying his fingers across my jeans and pressing me even closer to him. I flick my tongue against his, warm energy sizzling right through me. I want this moment to last forever.

But good things never do.

The sound of distant voices and laughter jerk us apart. I try to scramble off Mack, but he tightens his hold on me, lifting his head to see who might be coming.

"Let me go." I push against his shoulders.

"Why?" His frown is soft and curious.

"Because I don't want the attention. If people know we're together, everything's going to change. I don't…"

The worry scorching me obviously shows because Mack

runs his finger down my hairline with a soft smile and whispers, "Your secret is safe with me. I *promise* you. I'll never tell anyone."

I swallow. "I don't want people talking about me."

Mack gives me an ironic smile. "You're beautiful, you're foreign, you're mysterious. People are going to be talking about you whether you're with me or not."

I roll my eyes. "Yes, and you're cool, you're popular, and every girl in the school wants to get with you. If they see we're together, they're going to be talking about me even *more*. Now, let me go!" I slap his shoulder and he finally relents, loosening his grip...but only enough so that I still have to wrestle out of his grasp. It's a fighting chance, I suppose. I try to glare at him, but he just snickers and makes a silly face, which then gives me the giggles.

Honestly! I haven't laughed this much since I was a kid. No one's ever affected me the way Mack does.

I rise to my feet just as two familiar faces come around the corner. They're holding hands and looking adorable as their arms swing, chatting with each other, oblivious to the world around them. Tori says something to Colt, which makes him tip his head back in laughter and then wrap his arm around her neck. He pulls her close, burying his lips in her mounds of curls. She closes her eyes, resting her hand on his stomach and looking like she's been sent to Heaven.

Mack rises beside me, smirking as he watches the love-birds saunter onto the field. His fingers wriggle beneath my jacket, spreading across my lower back. Warm sizzles race up my spine and I lean back against him to enjoy the show.

Tori and Colt have stopped now and are gazing into each other's eyes. He's saying something that's making her cheeks turn fluorescent red. I snicker and look up at Mack. He grins, then gives me a sexy wink before letting out a loud wolf whistle.

Tori and Colt, who were about to kiss, jump apart from each other. Tori's grey eyes are large and sparkling while Colt's head tips to the side with a dry glare. He raises his middle finger at Mack, who returns the favor with a charming smile.

Boys.

I wave at Tori, who's still blushing like a strobe light. She tucks a curl behind her ear and takes Colt's hand as they walk toward us.

"We came here to get some privacy, dude. What the hell are you guys doing here?" Colt's eyes shift between us, the light bulb already coming on.

A tight knot forms in my stomach, but it's eased by the

feel of Mack's hand squeezing the nape of my neck, then pulling me against him. "We were looking for the same thing."

"Oh!" Tori's lips part. "Wow! Really?" Her smile is sunshine. I've never seen anybody's face light up so quickly. "That's so cool."

Okay, so we have a romantic in our midst. What's the bet she reads Jane Austen and watches rom-coms from the eighties…just like Eloise used to.

I swallow, thoughts of her pale, white face and red-rimmed eyes stealing my smile.

Colt points his finger between me and Mack. "So, I'm guessing this isn't public knowledge right now."

"Uh…" Mack gazes down at me, quietly asking the question we both have different answers to.

I give him a pleading look. He responds with a reluctant grin. "Yeah, we're keeping it quiet."

"Not a bad idea." Colt raises his eyebrows, sharing a silent message with Mack that's easy enough to interpret. He's dating someone who doesn't fit the mold… and it's not always easy.

I don't have to imagine how protective Colt must feel; it's obvious in the way he holds Tori to his side. I've watched them in the cafeteria. I've seen the glares he's shot Roxanne Carmichael and her snobby friends.

Heck, I've even seen the glares he's fired at other guys for simply looking at Tori. Oh yeah, he's got it bad for the pixie girl. I think that's what they call her.

"So, how's the weekend going?" Mack's still holding me against him like we've been a couple for years. I have to say, it's actually kind of nice to be standing here, the four us—two couples both trying to guard their relationships. Admittedly, mine and Mack's is only a newborn, but those are the ones you have to take extra special care of, right?

"Yeah, good." Tori bobs on her toes. "Colt's been teaching me to play Madden." She looks at me. "It's this PlayStation football game and I pretty much suck." Her lips dip into a resigned pout but break back into a smile when she looks up at her boyfriend. "But it doesn't help that I'm competing against the world's best player."

"Pffft." Mack snorts. "World's best player. Whatever."

"Shut up, man. I could kick your ass any day of the week." Colt grins.

"Bring it on, horse boy."

I laugh, enjoying the banter between them. It's so obvious how much they love and respect each other. They're acting like my brothers do—macho insults veiling a hard-core devotion. These two have 'lifelong friendship' written all over them.

Once again, my thoughts fire to Eloise and I'm reminded how fragile life can be. I turn into Mack, wrapping my arm around his waist and pressing my head to his shoulder. I don't care that Tori and Colt are watching. I need to cherish this moment.

Mack runs his arm down my back. "Kiwi Girl's been trying to teach me how to play rugby."

"No way, really?" Colt's eyes light, the blue fire in them almost mesmerizing.

"Yeah, he's not very good yet." I wink at Tori, who laughs.

"Well, maybe I need a better coach."

I slap his chest, wrinkling my nose at him. "I'm probably the best rugby coach in the state of Idaho!"

"You're probably the *only* rugby coach in the state of Idaho."

"Exactly!" I giggle. "Which is why I am the best."

Mack laughs at me before kissing the end of my nose and giving me a smile that turns my insides to hot mush.

Colt bobs on his toes like a kid at the counter of a candy shop. "Mind if we join?"

"Sweet as." I nod. Pulling away from Mack, I jog over

to the ball, picking it up and sending a perfect spiral pass to Colt. My dad would be proud.

Colt catches the ball against his side, his smile wide with approval.

I place my hands on my hips and smirk at Mack. "Now, that's how you pass, mate."

———

We spend the next hour mucking around with the ball. Even Tori gets in on the action. Now, *she's* a*dork*able, fumbling the ball and tripping over herself. Colt's there with a quick rescue every time, hauling her up like she weighs nothing. To him, she probably does. The way he lifts her over his shoulder and swings her in the air, you'd think she was made of feathers.

I love that.

I love that even though I'm not small and delicate like Tori, Mack can make me feel like a ballerina. He may not be the biggest guy on his team, but he's freaking strong. And maybe it's the fact that I'm still recovering from what happened back in New Zealand, I'm not sure, but I find Mack's strength a necessity. Like how did I ever live without it before? I've only experienced the full force of it over this weekend, but it's made me feel more safe and secure than I have in weeks. All this time, I've tried to be strong on my own, harboring my shame in silence. Now I've finally let someone in, and it's a huge relief. I want to cling to him, wrap myself inside the protection he's so willing to offer.

If only I could.

On Monday, as I'm carrying my tray out of the cafeteria line, I catch Mack staring at me. Our eyes connect and his rich brown gaze warms to a hot cocoa color that makes me want to fling the tray over my shoulder and run into his lap. Instead, I grip the plastic and swivel toward Anderson's table. He's still pissy with me for ditching him the other day…and basically being non-existent over the weekend.

"I thought you were here to hang out and see Idaho, not play a disappearing act," he'd complained when I got home last night. His voice had been kind of whiny and irritating, reminding me of Anna on a bad day.

I didn't tell him I'd been with Mack. Actually, I told him I'd been hanging out with Tori. He seemed to swallow that news okay, like Tori was an acceptable friend or something. He was acting like a bloody father figure. It took major resistance on my part not to flip him off and tell him that the cheerleaders obviously weren't the only snobs in this school, but I pressed my lips together and went to bed.

If I walk my butt over to Mack's table right now, it'll aggravate the shit out of Anderson. I still have to live with the guy for another month, and I'm all about avoiding angst at the moment. Plus, Roxy and her cheer-dettes probably won't be able to stomach it, either. Her icy blue eyes drill holes in the back of Mack's head while he's watching me. He may have been unaware of it, but I felt it before I even noticed it. I guess when you've been someone who's thrown those kinds of glares around, you're hyper aware of the vibes.

I want to tell them all to stick it, then lock lips with Mack right in front of everyone. But I won't. I can only imagine the buzz that would resonate throughout the school if we let on how we really feel about each other. I could definitely do without the gossip.

As boring as playing it safe is, it's all I can cope with right now. What I have going with Mack is too precious to throw into the fire.

So against every desire inside me, I set my tray next to Anderson Foster's and take a seat.

23

EYE CONTACT

MACK

I HATE that she won't sit with me.

I understand why she won't, but I still hate it.

Over the weekend, she opened up a little more about her New Zealand school and the ugly rumors that spread like a virus after word got out about Eloise. I want to kick her ex-boyfriend's ass for doing what he did. She should have been able to trust him the most but he turned on her, reveling in the gossip, fueling it until she couldn't take the heat.

It drove her here.

To be honest, I should be thanking him, but the look in her eyes when she relived what happened... She's still haunted by it. I'm going to do everything in my power to make sure nothing at Nelson High can touch her. My protective instincts were working overtime as I held her close and let her cry against me. I wanted to wrap her in a bubble and keep her safe, which is why I kept her to myself all weekend. I did have to share her with Colt and Tori for a while, but that ended up being really cool.

I glance at Colt, who's sitting opposite me. His mouth is full of food, making his cheeks bulge, as he listens to Tyler going on about his hot and heavy weekend. I give Ty a skeptical frown, wondering how much of his antics are actually truth. I wouldn't be shocked to find out the guy's still a virgin. Usually the ones who boast the loudest are the most inexperienced. Colt swallows his mouthful and laughs, shaking his head at Tyler before rolling his eyes at me. I snicker and take a mammoth bite of my hotdog. Chewing down my food, I peek over my shoulder again. I can't help myself. Kaija is sitting next to Anderson. Her long locks of luscious hair swish as she looks up at him, a polite smile on her lips. I can only see her profile, but I can tell her smile isn't real. I've seen the genuine article, and it's stunning enough to knock a guy on his ass.

Colt taps my foot with his boot, clearing his throat and tipping his head toward the end of our table as I spin around to scowl at him. My eyebrows lift when I spot Roxy's blue gaze drilling into me. We make eye contact and her lips rise into the sultry smile she usually gives me before walking us into the bonfire shadows and making out with me. We've gotten pretty hot and heavy in the past. Hell, we nearly did it once, but for some reason I can never understand, I just wasn't feeling it, and backed off before going all the way. I sat in the grass puffing, trying to come up with a good excuse to walk away while her fingers roamed beneath my shirt. A small twist of irony actually saved me that night. I heard Layla yelling from the other side of the bonfire and rushed in with my standard rescue. Two guys were fighting for her affections and she wasn't strong enough to break it up. I took her home straight after that, and Roxy and I have never mentioned our *nearly all the way* moment again.

Gazing at the cheerleader's flirty face now, I can tell she's thinking about it. The way her eyes dip, and the way she bites her lower lip and glances back up. She wants me.

But I don't want her.

I'm not sure I ever really did. She's pretty and everything, but there's something lacking. There's no spark between us. Nothing more than mindless lust. I'm an eighteen-year-old guy. I should be all about that—because I always have been—but, for some reason, Kaija makes me want more. I want to get to know her, not just her body and what she feels like, tastes like. I want to know if these crazy feelings I have are grounded in something bigger than just physical attraction, just wanting to sleep with her. Because I can do that with anyone. And right now, I don't want to cross that bridge with her. Not yet. Maybe that makes me a total wuss, but I don't care. I'm tired of that game. I'm ready to see if there's something more to life than just hooking up with cheerleaders and random chicks who just wanna say they scored with Mack Mahoney.

I run my hand through my hair with a sheepish grin, my cheeks heating as I admit the true impact one look has had on me. Kiwi Girl must be some kind of magician, because she's captured me. I'm thinking the L-word already. This is insane!

It's a total mind-flip to go from someone who's all about the casual make-out session to someone who is borderline obsessed with one particular girl. She's stolen my heart, made me feel things I never thought I would. She's with me constantly, playing in the corners of my mind, endearing me with her charm and playful smile…those emerald eyes.

I'm about to glance over my shoulder again when I catch Colt's eye. His steady look reminds me to not be so obvious. Clenching my jaw, I focus all my attention on Finn and his rant about the evils of Miss Turner's chemistry class, the whole time picturing Kaija's face as she threw the rugby ball at Colt, then turned to me with a smirk. *"Now, that's how you pass, mate."*

A smile lights my lips. I rub my hand over my mouth to try and hide it.

I can't wait for another *rugby* session with my girl this afternoon. I would invite Colt to join again, but I don't want to share Kaija's attention, so I'm selfishly keeping my lips sealed. Man, I can't wait for the Christmas break to start. Only one more week to go and I can see her whenever I want…hopefully.

I catch a glimpse of wild, scrappy curls approaching us from the right. Tori bobs into view, her smile brilliant as she walks around the table and wraps her thin arms around Colt's neck.

"Hey, Pixie Girl." He only ever uses his soft, husky voice with her. It's kind of pathetic, but I can hardly talk. I've been dating Kaija less than a week and I'm totally whipped. Colt and Tori have been together for three months now.

She perches her chin on his shoulder. "We need to go finish that assignment."

His upper lip curls and he lets out a thin whining sound.

"Come on, you know it'll be worth it." She kisses his cheek.

He skims his fingers across her arm. "Why don't you come sit with me? I can finish eating. You can hang out. And we'll do the assignment tomorrow."

"It's due tomorrow." Her small fingers play with the collar of his jacket, her sweet smile still not enough to convince him.

Tori lets out a little sigh, looks to the ceiling, then start grinning like a vixen. Her eyes dance as she presses her hand to the side of his head and hides her whispers from us all. Her face is adorable, bright with mischief, and Colt's mouth falls open, his cheeks glowing with color.

He jerks to look at her, his hungry eyes drinking her in.

She bites her lower lip and wiggles her eyebrows.

Colt starts scrambling for his stuff, jumping out of his seat and grinning. "Sorry, guys, I gotta go." His arms wraps around her tiny waist while Tyler makes choking noises next to me.

"Dude, what'd she say? What's she going to do to you?"

Shaking his head, Colt laughs and bends his knees so Tori can jump on his back. She springs up with a giggle, wrapping her legs around him and kissing the side of his neck.

"Dude, don't leave me hanging!" Tyler shouts to the departing couple. "You better tell me after!"

Colt spins when he reaches the door. "In your dreams, man." He laughs, hitching Tori a little higher. The curls bounce around her head as she laughs and waves goodbye.

"Damn." Tyler throws his fork down. "Who knew Pixie Girl had it in her."

"It's only 'cause she's with the right guy," Finn murmurs. Trust him to be all romantic about it. I've never known the guy to have a girlfriend; hell, at one point, I thought he was gay, until I made the mistake of looking at him funny one day. His responsive glare could've cut through steel. He knew what I was thinking. His voice was dry and a little scathing when he set me straight. *Just because I'm not a man-whore doesn't make me gay. There's nothing wrong with waiting for the right girl.*

I mumbled an apology and we've never spoken about it again.

Finn is a good person, right down to his core, and I respect that about him. Now that I know what it feels like to meet the *right* girl, I totally get where he's coming from. Glancing down the table, I run my eyes over Roxy. She's talking with my sister and Michelle, waving her hands in the air and looking gorgeous...and surly. Her eyes dart to the cafeteria exit where Colt and

Tori just left. She mutters something else I can't hear, but I don't need to. It's obvious they're pissed that Tori has stolen one of *their* Raiders. It makes me kind of relieved that Kaija wants to keep our relationship under lock and key. If Roxy ever found out about it, I wouldn't put it past her to sabotage the whole thing.

24

BUSTED

KAIJA

CHRISTMAS HAS COME AND GONE. I didn't get to see Mack as much as I wanted to. It didn't help that the Fosters pulled me out of town and we had to travel nine and a half hours to visit Mr. Foster's family in Eugene, Oregon. We spent a whole week there, squished into this four-bedroom house with fifteen people, busting out the sides. I had to share a bed with Dana—not the worst thing in the world, aside from the fact that she talks in her sleep. Oh, the things that girl dreams.

Mum's still annoyed with me that I chose to stay stateside for Christmas. She just doesn't get it, and I'm not about to explain it to her. She thinks Eloise tried to kill herself in my bedroom because she was looking for a safe place to end her life. I chucked the note before anyone saw it. I'm the only one who knows the truth. Well, except for my closest friends, who made all the right assumptions and fired them at me like poison-tipped arrows.

Their comments on social media were heinous, not to mention the cartoons Kylie and Stefan drew. A stick figure with Xs for eyes is such a simple thing, right?

It's not.

Those pictures still torment me in my sleep.

Slipping my phone into my back pocket, I pull on my coat, shaking off thoughts of a land far away and focusing on the things I can control...like spending the afternoon and evening with Mack.

He kept me entertained with texts while I was away—the painful Christmas dinner with his blended family, the relief he feels at knowing he doesn't have to suffer New Year's Eve with Derek, as well. He invited me to a party, but the Fosters have already organized a thing and apparently their guests are all super excited to meet me, so I can't really get out of it. Hence the reason I'm sneaking away to see Mack today. We arrived back late last night and everyone is still in their pajamas. I quietly mentioned to Mrs. Foster this morning that I'd love a little time to myself after the busy festive season, and she thinks I'm off for a walk around the lake this afternoon. Thankfully, she's an introvert, so she totally understands where I was coming from.

I practically skip down the stairs, my insides giddy and light as I walk to Mack's house. He lives about four blocks away. I haven't been to his place before. He sent me a screenshot map this morning and it's pretty straightforward. Left out the driveway. Right at the end of the street. Another right at the McDonald's intersection, and then it's the second street on my left and the fourth street on my right.

"Left, right, right, left, right," I sing to myself as I pick up my pace.

I'm desperate to see him.

I know. It's lame and pathetic, but I've missed him. I can't wait to see him, touch him, breathe in his scent. I used to wonder when Hanson and I were going out if it was love, but it was nothing compared to whatever is going on inside of me right now. Is it too early to admit the L-word?

Oh man, in my head—my soul—I'm totally there, and the thought of leaving Mack in three weeks makes my heart do this weird spasm and then drop into my stomach. I don't know how I'm going to do it. I just know that I need to cherish every second I have with him.

I break into a run, pumping my arms and screaming

around the corner. The golden arches appear on my right and I race past them. By the time I reach Mack's street, I'm puffing like a dog, but I don't stop until I'm standing at his mailbox and gazing up at a lush place that looks like it's straight out of a home and garden magazine.

My lips part as I walk up the path. The lawn is immaculate, the small shrubs and trees lining the edge of the house trimmed to perfection and surrounded by mulch. The entrance has these two large pillars leading up to a big archway. I run my fingers along the rock work, wondering how much the place is worth. Pausing outside the double doors, I study the frosted pattern in the glass—intricate vines twisting around each other to create a rectangular frame. I'm about to press the bell when the door swings open and Mack is standing before me, looking all kinds of gorgeous. His dark eyes drink me in, lighting at the corners as he wraps his arm around my waist and hauls me into the house.

He lifts me off my feet and I wrap my legs around his waist, relishing his strength. It engulfs me, chasing away my afflictions. I press my smile against his lip, running my fingers into his thick locks as he twirls his tongue around mine.

"I've missed you," he murmurs against my lips.

"Me too." I pull back to gaze at him, loving the expression on his face. Grazing my hand down his jaw, I dip my index finger into his chin dimple and smile.

"Come on, I'll show you my room." He turns for the stairs, obviously having no intention of putting me down.

The feminist in me tells me to wrestle out of his grasp, but come on, he feels so good. He's carrying me up to his room like I weigh nothing more than a bouquet of roses. I don't care what your views on gender equality are, you can't beat this feeling.

Resting my forearms on his shoulders, I play with the edges of his hair until we shuffle through his doorway. He lets me go with a little grunt, and I land on his bed with a bounce. His hand catches my arm before I topple onto the floor. Then he nestles down beside me and wraps his arm around my shoulders.

"So, welcome to Room a la Mack."

I bob my head, scanning the minimally decorated space. The wallpaper is a deep navy with a pale blue trim. We're sitting on his double bed. The duvet is pulled tight and wrinkle free, his pillows stacked neatly at the head. A white set of drawers sits against the wall next to a bay window, and the only clutter I see is a few picture frames on his dresser and a neat pile of paperwork on his desk.

So the guy likes it tidy. Nice. I like that. I don't know how people study with mess all around them.

I give him an approving smile and stand from the bed, walking over to his desk and running my finger along the straight edge. My eyes catch a stack of glossy pamphlets tucked between two textbooks and I instinctively reach for them.

Mack lets out a choking sound and lurches off the bed. "Make sure you put those back. Mom hasn't spotted them yet."

I scan the first one then flip it over to look at the next and the next and the next. They're brochures for colleges across the United States.

I hold them up. "Why don't you want your mum knowing?"

Mack sighs, gently taking them off me and shoving them back into his rather useless hiding place. "She's only interested in one college, and I applied for it months ago."

"Boise State University."

Mack clenches his jaw, sliding his hands into his pockets and staring down at the carpet. I watch his socked toes curl into the thick fabric.

"Maybe you should tell her you don't want to go."

"I can't." He huffs. "My future's set. It has been for years. This was always the plan, even before Dad died... It just became that much more important after he did."

I shrug, sliding off my jacket and hanging it over the end of his chair. "Plans can change."

"Not these plans," he mutters.

He starts drawing patterns in the carpet with his big toe. His biceps flex beneath his T-shirt while a tendon in his neck pings tight. It's like he's trying to hold it all in, keep it together for the sake of his family.

"I know your family has been through a lot, and it's obvious how much you care about them, but Mack..." I wait until he looks up at me before continuing. "It's *your* future. You should be able to make it whatever you want it to be."

His face crumples. "You don't get it."

"I do." I nod, stepping into his space and resting my hand on his taut arm. "But I'm telling you, the only person who has final say in your future is *you*. It's got to be your choice. You're the one who has to live it... and I want you to be happy."

A slow smile tugs at his mouth, pulling into a gorgeous grin as he grazes my cheek with the back of fingers.

"You know, when you say shit like that, you're in danger of making me fall in love with you."

I laugh, biting my lower lip and arching my eyebrow. "You're already in love with me. I think it's the kiwi accent that does it for ya. Or maybe it's the fact I come from a country where real men play real sports—you know, warrior dances before the game and all that." I wink.

His jaw works to the side as he fights a snicker and pulls me against his chest. "Or maybe it's those green eyes of yours...or the way your lips curve just here when you're trying not to smile." He presses his finger into the corner of my mouth, making my heart trip over itself. "Or it could be the shape of your..." His hand glides down my back, rounding over my butt.

"Oy, watch it." I slap his hand away and spin out of his grasp.

He captures my wrist before I can fully get away, gently pulling me back to his side. "Or it could be the way you say 'oy.'"

Mack cuts off my laughter with his warm mouth. It nestles over mine, working like a magnet to close the gap between us. I press myself against his chest, wrapping my arms around his neck and delving into the sheer ecstasy that is his mouth. His lips are soft, melding to mine, his tongue firm and in command, coaxing me into a deeper kiss that sends tendrils of pleasure racing down my body.

Shuffling us backwards, Mack leads me to the bed. The second his knees hit the edge, we flop onto it. In a fluid move that gives away Mack's experience, he spins me onto my back. I'm hardly one to judge and quickly shove the thoughts from my mind. I don't want to know which girls he's had in here before. I don't want to think about the guys in my past. It doesn't matter.

None of them exist in our future.

I dig my fingers into his hair, wrapping my leg around his knee. His hand glides up my thigh, squeezing my hip before wriggling beneath my shirt.

"Well, well, well, who have we got here?" A voice I don't recognize shatters the moment.

Mack jumps off me like he's been electrocuted. I perch up on my elbows and take in the sharp-faced guy checking me out. He's got one of those faces where his cheeks sink in a little, making his strong cheekbones and angular jawline even more severe. His dark eyes are small and gleaming, making the skin on the back of my legs crawl.

"You ever heard of knocking, Dickman?"

He smirks. "No, what is that?"

"Get out." Mack's voice is low and gruff as he straightens his shirt.

"I'm Derek." He stares at me, making no attempt to hide the fact he's checking out my boobs.

I clear my throat and tip my head with a droll glare. "Hi, Derek." I punch out the K, hoping it's obvious that I'm seriously unimpressed. Mack's told me all about this ball-bag.

He crosses his arms, the glint in his eyes sparking bright. "What's your name?"

"None of your business," Mack growls, stalking across the room and standing in front of him.

"Ooo, a mystery girl. How enticing." The way his eyes glitter makes me wonder if he's on speed or something. No one's eyes should be that glittery.

I get the impression that Mack will have to manhandle him from the room if Derek doesn't get the answers he's looking for. I'm not looking to cause a fight, so I sigh and say, "The name's Kaija."

"The accent's cute."

"Get lost!" Mack gets in his face, pointing at the open door.

"Alright, alright. Chill your kicks, big man." Derek's voice is dripping with scorn. I want to stand up and punch him one. The jealous little turd has nothing on Mack. His eyes swing back to me. His leering gaze makes me want to take a bath. "It's nice to meet you, Kaija."

"I wish I could say the same." I give him a polite smile while Mack snickers.

Derek's head jolts back, his eyebrows rising. "Wow, you guys make the perfect couple. Assbutts unite."

Mack's shoulders tense, his fingers curling into fists. I can sense him getting ready to grab Derek by the shirt and haul him out of the room. I'm inclined to let him, but a much sweeter voice arrives in the doorway, forcing Mack to take a step back.

"What are you doing here?" Layla frowns up at Derek, her disdain obvious.

"Hey, sis." He grins.

"I'm not your sister." She brushes past him but stops short when she sees me lying on her brother's bed. I try to smile at her, but can tell it's the wrong move. Her wide eyes narrow into fine slits, her bracelets clinking as she crosses her skinny arms. "What the hell are you doing on Mack's bed?"

Derek chortles. "Do you really need to ask?"

"Shut up!" Mack thunders.

"Are you kidding me?" Layla's dark brows dip together as she gives her brother an incredulous glare.

"Layla!" I can't see Mack's face, but I assume he's scowling. He sounds like he is.

After a short beat, she goes all innocent, her eyes widening.

"What?" She shrugs and puts on a *pity me* voice. "You said you were going to drive me to the mall tonight."

"Ask one of your friends to take you. Or better yet, get your driver's license!"

Layla's baleful glare tells me that's an ongoing argument. She clears her throat and sticks her chin in the air.

"Mom grounded me after my last detention. If you go with me, I'll get away with it."

"I'm not taking you to the mall," Mack snaps.

Layla gives him a sulky frown before glancing down at her powder-blue nail polish. "Well, what am I going to do tonight?" Her tone has a mocking lilt to it. "I know! I'll text Roxy." She pulls out her phone. "I'm sure she can give me some ideas. And you know she'll be so interested to find out Kaija's here. She really wants to be friends." Her sticky sweet voice drips with insincerity, her threat so lightly veiled it's actually pathetic. That little cow.

Mack's neck stiffens, his biceps flexing as he makes two fists.

Layla starts tapping her phone screen.

It doesn't take more than ten seconds for Mack to lurch forward and clamp his hand around Layla's tiny fingers. "You know you can really be a little tart-fart."

She bites her lips against a grin and I get the distinct feeling he's called her that before.

Spinning around, he gives me an apologetic smile. His eyes flash with that same old question: *Is it time to stop hiding our relationship?*

I shake my head, about to say how much I love shopping at the mall, but then I spot Layla's face. She so does not want me tagging along. Her dark eyes flash with a look I've seen a hundred times before, and I don't trust her not to do something to seriously screw up what Mack and I have going. I'm the girl who's making her brother act differently. He's dating a girl who doesn't fit the mold, and she doesn't like it.

I can see quite clearly that Miss Layla won't just step aside and take it if Mack doesn't play the way she wants him to. He's told me a little about her background, how much her father's death affected her. But in this moment, I can't help wondering if Mack's just a big old softy and Layla's playing him like a freaking violin.

Although I'm inclined to call her a bitch and tell her she can't manipulate us this way, I'm also not stupid. Mack and I are on limited time, and I don't want our last three weeks to be ruined by a high school bitch-fest. If she brings *her girls* in on the action, we're totally screwed.

"You know what, um…" I run my tongue over my top teeth. "I actually have to get going."

Mack's eyebrows dip. "No, you don't."

"The Fosters are expecting me for dinner." I try to convey what I'm thinking with a look, but Derek opens his stupid mouth and cuts me off.

"I'll walk you home."

Mack spins, moving to the side to create a solid barrier between me and his stepbrother. Derek snickers and tries to move over so he can eye me up again, but Mack blocks his view.

"Feeling a little territorial, I see. Are you gonna go piss on her now, so we all know she's yours?"

Mack snarls—like, seriously, he sounds like a wolf ready to rip Derek's vocal chords out. Jumping off the bed, I hurry towards him, running my hand down his arm and pressing my cheek against his shoulder.

"Thanks for the offer, Dick…sorry, Derek, but Mack and Layla can drop me home on their way out." I look to Layla, who's fighting a grin. I think she liked my 'dick' faux pas. "If that's okay with you?"

"Sure." She nods, gifting me a smile that could be genuine—it's hard to tell.

I grin back at her, then squeeze Mack's hand, hoping to wipe the look of dark disappointment off his face.

"I'm just going to go change." Layla spins out of the room, Derek following in her wake.

As soon as we're alone, Mack turns to me, opening his mouth with what I'm sure will be a heated protest. I press my finger over his lips. "You didn't see her face behind your back. I'm just playing it safe."

Mack frowns. "We shouldn't have to play it safe."

"I know these girls. I used to be one of them. Trust me, if you value what we've got going here…" I tip my head with a pleading look.

His shoulders droop with a heavy sigh, so I wrap my arms around him and touch my lips against his ear, whispering an idea I had when I was driving back from Oregon yesterday. I feel his cheeks rise with a grin and his arms tighten around my waist.

"I'll be there," he murmurs, then kisses the crook of my neck.

25

A NEW YEAR'S BUBBLE

MACK

I DRIVE, taking the longest route possible back to the Fosters' place. Layla notices and starts huffing in the back seat. I ignore her and focus on chatting with my girl. I pull up to the curb a couple of houses down from Roxy's place, making sure no one's watching when I kiss Kaija goodbye. When she opens her door, the interior light comes on and I flash her a look filled with heat and yearning.

She smiles and mouths, "See you later." Her wink is sexy as hell.

She shuts the door and starts running for the Fosters' place, cutting the corner of the Carmichaels' lawn. Her long hair swishes from side to side and I can't wait to run my fingers through it again.

"Finally," Layla mutters, hopping over the parking brake and thumping into the passenger seat.

I accelerate forward, driving slowly past the Fosters' to make sure Kaija got inside safely. The door is just closing as we pass, so I press the gas, picking up speed.

"Thank God that's over." Layla clips her seatbelt then runs a hand through her long hair.

"Did you really have to be so rude to her?"

"Probably not." She grins at me, her tongue poking out the side of her mouth.

I huff and glare at her but she's looking out the side window, unaware of my angsty vibes.

I should be mad at her. I should be kicking her out of my car and yelling, "Screw the mall! You can walk home." But I can't. Because I suck at saying no to Layla. I've been looking after her ever since Dad got sick. It's become a habit, I guess. And when he died, the urge to protect her only grew, especially when Derek became part of the family.

Ditching girls to hang out with my sis has never been a problem before...but it's different now. I really care about my Kiwi Girl, and I won't have Layla shitting all over it.

"I like her, you know. Way more than I've ever liked anybody."

Layla's shoulders ping tight, her nostrils flaring. "Whatever."

I clear my throat, accelerating through the four-way crossing, then taking the next left. I'm not ready to drop my Kaija conversation, but Layla launches into details for tomorrow night before I get a chance to say more.

"So, the party's near Westhaven Mall. I say we leave around nine. That'll get us there with a couple of hours to party before the big countdown."

"I have to leave at eleven," I murmur.

"What?" Layla snaps. "You can't leave before midnight. It's New Year's Eve!"

I sniff, avoiding eye contact as I guide the car toward the mall. "I've got somewhere I need to be."

Layla groans, tipping her head back. "Please tell me you're not ditching early so you can go hook up with the foreign girl."

"She has a name!"

"Give me a break, Mack. You're not this guy."

"What guy?"

"The guy who's whipped! Girls come to *you*. That's the way it works. You kiss. You make their night and then…"

I'm already shaking my head, the idea of sucking face with random girls suddenly unappealing. "Not this time."

"Why?" Layla's bracelets clink as she flicks her hands in the air. She looks at me like I've started drinking crazy juice for breakfast.

"She's different." I shrug. "You don't know her."

"I know that she's not the kind of girl you usually go after. She hangs out with Nerd Squad. Seriously, Mack, do you care nothing for your reputation?"

I hit the brake, jerking to a stop at the red light before turning to my sister. She's sounding scarily like Roxanne Carmichael right now. My brows dip together as I frown at her. "When it comes to her, I couldn't give a shit about my rep."

"Yeah, right." She rolls her eyes. "Come on, you're Nelson High's most eligible guy. You pride yourself on that. You get off on being the one everybody wants."

"That's total bullshit," I mutter, wishing her words didn't sting so bad. The ring of truth pinging off them is deafening. I don't want to be that guy anymore. I'm sick of living up to everybody's expectations. I want to apply to whatever college I feel like. I want to walk into Nelson High without half the student body looking to me for guidance! I just want to...

"I don't get it. She's so...not you."

"She's not as different as you think." I grip the wheel, wishing the words hadn't slipped out so easily.

Layla whips her head to study me, her keen eyes drilling holes through my forehead. "What do you mean?"

"Nothing." I shake my head. "She's just... She understands...us. She knows...the kind of people we are."

Shit, I'm doing a lousy job of trying to stand up for my girl and cover for her at the same time.

Layla goes quiet beside me.

I let the silence simmer between us, hoping she'll drop it and move on.

"When does she leave to go back to Hobbit land?" Layla's voice is soft, reminding me of the sweet girl that lies beneath her layers of makeup and defensive shielding.

I wish she didn't have to be like this. I want to wrap my arm around her and tell her that it's okay to feel afraid and cry over Dad. Putting on this false façade won't make the pain go away. Sometimes I wonder if she's going to have to hit rock bottom before realizing all of this. Kind of like Kaija did.

My breath hitches at the thought. I can only imagine

Layla's reaction to something that horrifying. Kaija's got a quiet strength that Layla's never had. My sister's suffered enough. There's no way she'd cope with rock bottom…which is probably why I'm always so protective of her.

My muscles tense and my wrist bone pops as I clench the wheel and accelerate with the green light. "We've got three weeks left."

"So things will go back to normal soon enough," she mumbles to herself, sounding relieved.

A deep sadness that I haven't had the courage to unearth yet settles inside of me, gnawing at my core. "I don't think I'll ever be normal again, Lay-lay."

I turn on my left blinker and pause to check the intersection before glancing at my sister. Her large eyes are filled with a mixture of fear and sadness. Layla's never done well with change. Which is probably why she's not coping with the whole me and Kaija thing.

But I can't let that stop me, can I?

For the first time in my life, I've found something I want…I mean *really* want. Should I have to give that up for the good of the family?

It doesn't seem fair.

But since when has life ever been about fair?

The music blasts out of the house, trying to reel me back in, but I won't let it. I have better things to do. I jiggle the keys in my hand as I run for my car. It's 11.05pm. I've got plenty of time to make it to the football field before midnight. A smile tips my lips before I can stop it; there's this weird energy buzzing through me.

Layla's in the thick of the party, dancing with Roxy and Michelle. I made her promise me not to tell anyone where I was going. I took her to the damn mall like she wanted me to, and my threatening voice as I towered over her was enough to make her mutter, "Okay, okay. I promise."

Right now, the three of them are giggling like hyenas, oblivious to me sneaking out the door. I figure my sister is safe enough hanging out with her girls. It's better than seeing her draped all over some guy, which is her usual style. I made Michelle promise to get Layla home safely. Finn and Tyler are there, as well, and I made them swear not to let her up to any of the bedrooms. Colt passed on tonight, wanting to spend it with Tori instead. I finally get why. Before meeting Kaija, I would have called him dead rubber for ditching us and told him to bring her along, but he's got a girl to protect and although she comes to some stuff, the big parties like this are snake pits—dripping fangs and poisonous bites waiting around every corner. When guys like Quaid Miller could turn up at any moment and girls like Roxy arrive with their claws already showing, it's better to keep the little Raider's thief out of the action.

I'm confident Kaija can handle that kind of thing; she's not sweet and innocent like Pixie Girl. But I don't want to put her in the position where she has to fight. She's trying to turn over a new leaf, and putting her back into Catty-ville is not going to help her do that.

I drive too fast on the way to the stadium. Thankfully, I'm not drunk; knowing I had to leave early made me reach for Coke instead of beer. Thoughts of Kaija have been dancing in my brain all day. I laugh like an excited chimp as I pull the car into the parking lot and lurch out the door. Locking it with a beep, I stuff the keys in my pocket before checking my watch again. I've got ten minutes to be standing centerfield. I dash inside and find the space empty. Tucking my hands into my jacket pocket, I saunter across the grass. It's cold, and puffs of white mist light the air every time I breathe out.

The stadium is eerily quiet. I do a slow spin and picture the stands filled with cheering people. They're on their feet, chanting, "Raiders! Raiders!" It's weird to think it's over now. It's weird to think the next time I pull on a uniform it'll be for the Boise State Broncos.

That thought should excite me, right?

So why does it feel like a heavy rock in the pit of my stomach?

Restless, I check my watch again. There's only a minute until midnight and Kaija's not here. I frown. Maybe she couldn't get away. Is it pathetic that I'll be totally gutted if she doesn't make it?

"Ten! Nine!"

I spin at the voice hollering at me from the gate.

Kaija laughs, swiveling to get through the opening before running across the field. "Eight! Seven!" White breaths are popping out of her mouth too. I grin, still able to capture her stunning smile in the moonlight. I love the way her long hair flies behind her back as she speeds toward me.

"Six! Five!" I call.

She's closing the gap between us and I can now see the sparkle in her vibrant eyes.

"Four." She puffs. "Three." She stops in front of me, reaching for my jacket and curling her fingers into it.

"Two…" I slide my fingers across her cheek, burying them in her silky locks. "One…" I lean toward her and whisper, "Happy New Year."

"Happy New Year," she whispers back before meeting my mouth with a kiss so warm and luscious it steals the chill from the air and turns it into a summer night.

I can almost feel the bubble forming around us, enclosing us in a perfect start to the year. I don't want to think about three weeks from now. I don't want to think about football…or college…or any of that crap. I just want to focus on this moment, this bubble shielding Kaija and me from the outside world.

26

POP!

KAIJA

THE WORD 'MONDAY' can sometimes be treated like a cursed word, can't it? The connotations surrounding the first workday of each week are often bad and people grumble their way out of bed. Not me. This morning, I practically bounce to the bathroom, brushing my teeth with a smile on my face, singing in the shower, getting dressed with a giggle.

It's kind of lame, to be honest, but I'm just so happy.

The holidays are over and I'm going to see Mack today. We've got just under three weeks left together before I fly back to New Zealand, and I want to spend as many seconds as I can with him. On New Year's Eve, we kissed until our noses were frozen. Then Mack drove me home, and we kissed some more in his car. I would have spent all weekend doing that with him, but the Fosters wanted to take me sightseeing. Dana managed to get out of it because she had a monster assignment that had been due *before* the Christmas break. Her punishment was to stay home and work. Lucky thing. I had to spend the last weekend of the holiday hiking through the icy snow at Yellowstone National Park. Admittedly, it was beautiful, but all I could think about was Mack.

I have never been this hung up on someone before. It's ridiculous how giddy, dizzy, and light I feel. It's like floating in a bubble of happiness and waving down at the bullshit below. Can't touch me.

With a big grin, I skip down the stairs and out the door, my boots crunching over the light snow as I make my way to Mrs. Foster's car. She's already got the heater running. I slip into the back seat and grin at Dana. She gives me a twitchy smile, curling her fingers around her binder.

"Did you get your assignment done?"

"Uh-huh." She bobs her head, then bites her lip.

I nudge her with a playful smile and whisper, "When is it due in?"

"Fifth period."

"Sweet as. You can finish it off at lunchtime. Your mum

will never figure out you spent the weekend watching movies."

Her eyes bulge.

"I thought so." I wink at her. "Don't worry. I won't tell."

Her giggle is short and jittery. She swallows a squawking sound and bites her lips together. Anderson's jacket rustles as he looks over the seat and tries to smile. He's still mad at me for sneaking out of the New Year's Eve party. I think he was hoping for a midnight kiss. I haven't told him I went to see Mack, but I'm sure he's guessed it. He didn't say anything while we were away this weekend—well, not about Mack anyway. He was too busy talking about everything else under the sun. I never knew there was so much to learn about the geological features of Yellowstone National Park. Who needs a ranger when you've got Anderson Foster by your side?

Mrs. Foster stops the car outside school. We all jump out and mumble our goodbyes.

"I'm at work all day today, so if you need anything, call me at the office first!" she calls. We all wave in acknowledgement, then turn for the school.

I scan the parking lot for Mack's car, but don't see it straightaway. It could be hiding behind a bigger vehicle.

I hope so. He's probably waiting for me at my locker. I try to temper my glee.

"Oh, there's Amy. I'm just going to ask her if she's finished her AP English essay." Anderson veers away from us, heading for the blonde whose thumbs are flying over her phone screen.

I grin down at Dana and roll my eyes. "Do you ever worry what will happen if he *doesn't* make valedictorian?"

My short companion titters then races up the school steps, hurrying left as soon as she walks through the door. She's obviously freaking out about her overdue assignment. I spin at the top of the steps but don't spot Mack's blue and orange Camaro. There's still fifteen minutes before the homeroom bell, so he'll probably arrive any minute. I'm tempted to wait for him, but decide that really crosses the pathetic, swooning girl-friend line, so I force myself inside to get ready for my first class.

The bounce in my step doesn't falter until I notice that the white sheets of paper lining the walls seem to converge at my locker. I'd been too busy toying with the idea of boldly greeting Mack with a kiss to actually take note of what was on the advertisements. But the sheets are plastered all over my locker, like it's the queen's hive and all the notices have spawned from there. With a bemused frown, I approach to get a better view.

The second I draw near enough to read the fine print, my heart lurches in my chest, like someone's slashing it in half with a machete.

Cartoon drawings cover the pages on display—little stick figures with Xs for eyes and speech bubbles filled with all the gossip I tried so hard to escape back in New Zealand.

With trembling fingers, I snatch the top sheet free, the paper ripping as I tug against the tape holding it there.

The whole story's there—me taunting Eloise, her crying, me handing her a bottle of pills (yeah, that rumor started just before I split), and then her…dead on my bed. It's all been drawn out in cartoon form, in the exact same style Kylie and Stefan used.

"What the hell?" I whisper. The acid burning my brain is making it hard to think straight.

All I can focus on now are the thick, ugly words scrawled across the bottom of the page.

We know who you really are. Go back home, you murdering little slut!

I can't compute what's going on right now.

My deepest, darkest secret is on full display, but my

mind is thrumming with one thought—Mack's the only one who knew about this.

If he was after the ultimate prank—he got it.

He totally played me. I fell for his charm, his smile, those lips! And I handed him ammo by the bucket load.

Tears scorch my eyes as I scrunch the sheet of paper and hurl it at the lockers. My lips quiver and I have to fight the feral cry rising inside of me. Lurching forward, I rip the damning sheets off until I'm standing in a pile of paper shreds. But it's a pointless maneuver, because the second I turn around, all eyes are on me.

And not just that. They're all holding white sheets of paper covered in cartoons.

Stick figures with Xs for eyes.

The air in my lungs is like a thick fog—icy and impossible to breathe. I stumble away from the horrified stares, nearly tripping as I skid on the polished floor.

Someone catches me, hauling me to my feet. His hands are strong and sure. Part of me wants to surrender to his arms, but the wild anger storming through me shoves him away.

Anderson stumbles back, his eyes wide with shock and revulsion. I blink, suddenly realizing that I'm staring at my host brother, not the guy I thought I loved.

The paper in his hand is shaking as he holds it up to me. "Is this true? Did you drive someone to commit suicide?"

I snatch the sheet out of his hand and push past him, fighting the sob desperate to burst out of my throat. I won't give in. Mack will not see me cry. That asshole!

Rounding the corner, I spot Amy and Tori coming towards me. They're looking at the sheet of paper too. Tori's skin is pale, making her freckles stand out. Amy is shaking her head with a sharp frown on her face.

They lurch to a stop when they see me, and Tori's grey eyes fill with a sympathy that's going to make me cry. "Who would do this to you?" She steps closer to me. "I mean, they're total lies...right?" The doubt on her face makes me take a step back. I can't answer her. I can't lie to this girl. She can see the truth on my face anyway. Her lips part and she starts blinking, then jerks her head to look at Amy.

I can't do this.

Spinning the other way, I run, aware of every eye on me, of every scandalous whisper rocketing down the hall. Taking a right, I head for the exit, ready to make my big escape, and nearly barrel straight into Roxy and her pack of cheerleaders. Layla glances up and sees me gaping at her. Her eyes round and she looks back at the sheet Roxy's holding, like she's just been punched in the guts.

Roxy snickers, then looks up with a smirk. "Well, well, well. Isn't this interesting? I knew there was something off about you." She shakes her head and I take off before she can say anything else.

Tears are building inside me, pressing against my inner walls, threatening to pop out of me like a frickin' geyser. But I won't let them.

I can't.

Thumping down the steps, I nearly slip on the ice, but catch myself before ass-ing over in front of everyone outside. They don't know yet. They haven't seen the slander covering the halls. But it won't be long. Soon my name will be slathered in mud.

I spot Mack sauntering up the path with Colt and Finn in tow. They're laughing about something but they all stop and turn as Tyler hollers at them to wait up. He vaults the fence and jogs over to them, his dimples on display.

Was it him? Did he help Mack photocopy these shitty drawings and paste them up all over the school?

I thunder towards Mack, slapping the sheet into his chest before cracking him across the cheek with my icy-cold fingers.

"Well done! You went for the long con. Nicely played."
I spit the words at him, rage making them jerk and trip
out of my mouth. "You're fucking brilliant, Mack! Is
that what you want me to say?"

He's standing there gaping at me, red fingermarks
scoring his pale skin.

Colt and Finn have taken a step back, giving us some
space while Mack slowly recovers from my attack,
collecting the sheet of paper off the ground and gazing
down at it.

His face crumples with a frown, then his eyes pop wide
with horror.

"You piece of shit!" I push his chest. He doesn't even
have the courtesy to stumble backwards. Damn his
stupid strength. "I trusted you!"

I'm screaming now, which won't be helping my cause,
but what the hell. It's a completely failed cause anyway.
I'll never be able to escape my heinous past.

People are staring at us. I can feel their affronted gazes
from every angle, surrounding us, judging me. No
doubt feeling sorry for Mack.

"How could you do this to me?" I choke out the words,
the tears threatening to reveal themselves in ugly,
stomach-wrenching sobs.

"Kaija, I didn't... I didn't do this."

I shake my head, backing away when he reaches out for me. "You were the only one who knew."

"I didn't do this." His words are whispered in desperation, the agonized look on his face begging me to believe him.

I can't.

It's too dangerous.

There's only one move I can make here.

I shove past Mack and I run.

27

TEAR DOWN

MACK

"KAIJA!" I drop my bag and chase after her. As usual, she makes me work for it. I pump my legs a little harder and finally manage to grab her arm before she reaches the end of the path.

"Let go of me!"

She thumps my arm, but I refuse to loosen my grip, instead dragging her against my chest.

"Stop!" She shoves and strains until I'm forced to step back. But I won't release my hold.

I bend down so we're eye-to-eye. "I didn't do this!"

"Then who the hell did? You're the only one who knew!"

"I don't know, okay? But I'm gonna find out."

"Oh, whatever! Like it's going to make any difference now." She wrenches her arm, trying to loosen my grip, but I won't give in. How can she assume it's me? Does she not believe how much I care about her?

Anger sparks within, no doubt fueled by a foreboding fear.

"Would you stop struggling? I'm not letting you go!"

"That's not your choice. It's over, Mack! Now get your hands off me!" She's screaming in my face, her eyes wild and unrecognizable.

"How can you think I would do this to you?"

"I obviously don't know you as well as I thought. Maybe you and Layla are in on this together. You're acting like you give a shit about me just to cover her ass."

"Don't bring my sister into this."

"Are you blind? She wants me out of the picture. If it wasn't you, maybe it was her. How'd she wrangle the truth out of you, huh? What little manipulation did she play? Or did Roxy put you up to this? Is she in on it too? Maybe Finn? Tyler? Oh, or maybe Sam. I know how much she likes a good joke."

Her words are little arrows, hitting me with their

poison tips and igniting my anger. "What? Of course not! Don't be ridiculous."

"Oh? Now I'm being ridiculous? Because my entire life —my deepest secret—was just plastered all over the school, a secret only *you* knew about, and that makes me ridiculous?"

"That's not what I meant." I huff.

"I'm done with this," Kaija says. "With this stupid school. With trying to put this behind me. With trusting people." Her eyes lock onto mine and all I see is cold disdain. "And I'm done with you."

"What? What are you talking about?" It feels like a knife blade through my stomach. Those eyes that captured me are now trying to slice me to shreds.

"I'm finished. *We're* finished."

A pain I've never felt before ripples through my ribcage. "Just like that? You're just giving up on us? All because of this?"

"There is no us," she says bitterly. "Every mate for himself."

"Kai—"

Her expression folds with a fleeting look of grief before hardening at the edges. Her green eyes swirl with anger and she uses my lapse in concentration to rip her arm out of my grasp.

"It never would have lasted anyway," she murmurs.

I stare at her in shocked silence, still trying to wrap my brain around what the hell she's saying to me. Her lower lip trembles as her eyes begin to glisten. She then lets out this whimpering kind of breath, spins on her heel and starts hauling ass down the footpath.

It takes me a second, but I chase after her, calling her name. Her words destroyed me. Her belief that I was somehow involved should have me turning away from her, but I can't let her go. Not like this. Not ever.

She's fast. I push harder, gaining ground, but she doesn't look back.

She screams around the corner and I yell her name again. "Kaija!"

I'm about to put on another burst of speed when my shoe hits a crack in the concrete and I hit the ground with a sharp hiss. I roll and spring back to my feet, ignoring the throbbing in my knee and elbow. My run ends up being more of a hobble. By the time I limp around the corner, she's gone.

"Shit!" I fist my hair, scouring the street for signs of which way she may have gone...but I see nothing. She's disappeared into thin air, and all I can do now is turn back to the guys.

I can't think past her soul-destroying words. Did she really mean them? Or was she still getting over the shock of what's just been done to her?

I'm going to kill whoever drew those damn pictures. Shoving my hands in my pockets, I stalk back to my friends who stood by, far enough away to witness everything, but not close enough to hear what went down.

"You alright?" Colt points to my knee.

I glance down at my ripped jeans and give him a short nod. The graze stings but it's not bad. It doesn't hurt at all compared to the aching in my chest.

"O-kay." The word slides out of Tyler's mouth as he points down the street. "So Kiwi Girl's gone a little cray-cray."

My death glare makes him snicker, his dimpled cheeks turning a hot red. He holds up the brutal sheet of paper. "This isn't true, is it?"

With a low growl, I snatch it from him and tear it in half before stalking into the school. The guys chase after me, their silent questions lashing me on the back.

I can't believe this.

Who the hell would do this to her?

Storming into the building, I notice a gaggle of freshman girls bunched around a sheet of paper. Their hushed whispers and wide eyes tell me everything I need to know. Marching over to them, I whip the sheet out of their hands and scrunch it into a tiny ball.

They all gasp in unison, the one closest to me shrinking away from my steam. "Stop reading that shit and get to class."

They scamper like rabbits, jumping away and scurrying around the corner. I follow their trail and notice a line of white sheets pinned to the wall. People are hovering in front of it, gasping and whispering.

"Is that the exchange student?"

"Yeah, the one who pranked the Raiders."

"Whoa, I thought she was nice."

"She *is* nice!" I yell, shoving them away and tearing the first sheet off the wall. "Get to class!"

"The bell hasn't rung yet," the guy beside me mutters.

I turn to him with flaring nostrils. He stumbles away from me, nearly tripping over his friend before recovering and shuffling down the hallway. The others pick up the hint and scatter, leaving me in peace so I can absorb the shitbomb that just exploded in our school.

The line of posters is endless, photocopy after photo-copy of the hideous comic. Kaija is portrayed as a stick figure with big boobs and long curly hair. The speech bubbles are filled with kiwi-isms, like someone's looked up 'kiwi slang words' on Google. I force myself to read through the eight boxes. They show Kaija to be a world-class bitch, taunting this meek girl until she's lying on a bed with Xs for eyes and pills scattered on the floor beside her. With a feral snarl, I start yanking the sheets off the wall, working my way down the hall, tearing and ripping, following the path of destruction. The bell rings, but I ignore it. By the time I reach Kaija's locker, the hallways are empty except for Colt, Tyler and Finn, who are working to tear down the last of the posters.

Kaija's locker was covered—I can tell by the leftover tape marks and the pile of ripped paper on the floor.

Go back home, you murdering little slut!

The words taunt me. How could someone write that? How the hell did anyone find out?

I can only imagine Kaija's horror as she walked into the school and saw this.

And she thought I did it.

"Shit!" I yell, smashing my fist into her locker.

The force of my punch brutalizes my knuckles, but I'm

too pissed to feel the pain. I slap my hands against the metal and force air to my brain. I'm so dizzy with outrage I can barely see through the haze.

I sense Finn's gaze and turn to glare at him. His dark eyes are calm, yet wary. He'll jump in if I go all ape-shit. Thankfully, everyone's in class, so the only people I can go after are my boys and they'll sack me before I hurt them.

I clench my jaw, trying to hide how riled I am. Kaija shared that intimate secret with me, poured out her heart, *trusting* that I wasn't going to tell anyone.

And I didn't.

"When I find out who did this…" I shake my head.

"We'll help you kick his ass." Tyler plants his feet beside me and crosses his arms.

I lean forward and rest my head on the cool metal. My hand is starting to throb, but I don't want to look at it.

"I'm really sorry, man," Finn murmurs.

"There's so much more to the story than this." My voice shakes, feeling Kaija's shame and humiliation. "I can't believe she thinks I'm responsible." I sound broken now. The rage is wearing off, replaced with a deep sadness that's cutting me in half. How could she have so little faith in me? Was everything I'd been feeling a freaking joke? I thought it was reciprocal, but...obviously not.

"Who would do this to her?" Colt's face is rumpled with concern. What's the bet he's thinking about Tori, trying to figure out how he can keep his girl safe from this kind of attack?

What the hell's he worried about? Tori's so clean she sparkles. But Kaija has a past...and she had every right to keep it a secret.

My brain is spinning with how it could have gotten out. Did she say something to someone else? Did Anderson Foster go through her room and unearth some nugget?

I slap the locker and stand tall. "I'm gonna kill him."

"Hey, slow down." Finn raises his hand at me, his long dark fingers stretching into the air. "Don't go making assumptions. You'll only make enemies out of the people who might be able to help you."

I grit my teeth, then huff. "I've gotta find out who did this."

"Retribution can wait." Finn jerks his head toward the end of the hallway. "You need to go find her first. Make sure she's okay."

"She doesn't want to be found. She just dumped me." I close my eyes and look to the ceiling.

"Aw, come on. That's bullshit," Colt murmurs. "I saw you guys together. You've got something going on. She's in shock right now. As soon as she's cooled off, she'll be able to see straight again. You need to be there when that happens."

"You have to try, bro." Finn slaps my shoulder. "Go on. We'll cover for you."

"Do you want me to come with?" Tyler, when he's acting serious, is as solid as a freaking redwood.

I give him a short, closed-mouth smile before shaking my head. "I've got to do this on my own. Can you just make sure, all of this"—I point to the paper on the floor—"is gone by the end of the day?"

"You got it, man." The guys all nod and Finn holds out his fist. I pound it, then hitch my bag onto my shoulder and take off for the parking lot. The sound of tapping feet in the hall forces me to duck into an alcove. Thankfully, the teacher doesn't spot me, and I sneak out while she walks away.

Tearing out of the school, I make a beeline for the Fosters' place. Surely that's where she would have gone. If it were me, I'd be hiding up in my room, punching pillows and shouting out every vile word I could think of.

All I can hope is that she copes with it in a similar way.

If she can have a scream-fest, it might calm her down enough to listen to me.

I'm not sure how I'm going to make her believe me. As I drive to her place, I can't think of any words that are right. How do you convince someone that you haven't betrayed them when you have absolutely no proof of your innocence?

The fact she thinks it might be Layla is eating at me too. My sister wouldn't go that far...would she? My doubts are growing with each passing minute, making me feel sick.

Slamming on the brakes, I bring the car to a swift stop outside the Fosters' place. The street is eerily quiet. Everyone's at work or school. I'm not used to being in the neighborhood when it's empty and I find it unnerving. Jumping out the door, I race up the path and start ringing the bell as soon as I can reach it.

"Kaija!" I holler, backing away from the door and looking up at the windows. I'm straining for signs of life, anything to indicate her presence.

Nothing.

The curtains don't move. What I think is her bedroom window doesn't slam shut, which means she's probably not up there. I study the drainpipe, wondering if I can climb up and look into the window. The gap is too small to squeeze through and there are probably safety locks keeping it ajar.

I run my hand through my hair with a frustrated groan, then pound on the door again.

"Kaija, come on! I've got to talk to you!"

Nothing.

I walk around the side of the house, peering in windows, but the longer I stay, the more I sense that no one is home. The Fosters' house is empty.

Which leaves me with only one question—where the hell is my girl?

28

TIME TO GO HOME

KAIJA

THE AIRPORT.

I usually love this place.

It's full of vibrant energy and has this busy atmosphere that's constantly buzzing—baggage trolleys, bustling people, hellos, goodbyes, cuddles, tears, laughter, and smiles. It all mixes together into one big melting pot to create the most fascinating place in the world. You can learn more about universal human behavior in one day at the airport than you can in six months of social sciences class. That's what I think anyway...and it's one of the reasons I love coming to the airport, any airport.

But not today.

Today, I hate the airport.

Unfortunately, it's the only place that's going to get me where I need to go.

Home.

That word normally fills people with warmth and comfort.

It tastes like ash in my mouth.

A lady's voice comes over the intercom. "Flight UA739 to San Francisco, now boarding at Gate 12."

I check my watch. I still have four hours before my flight departs. I tuck my backpack under my feet, hoping I remembered everything. Grabbing my stuff was a chaotic rush. I flew through the house like a tornado—snatching, yanking, stuffing. I no doubt left my crap scattered throughout the Fosters' home. I can't care about it. I just have to get out of here.

Trentham Domestic Airport is about a forty-minute drive from Nelson. The cab fare was ridiculous, but I paid it anyway. What choice did I have?

Thankfully, the guy at the United Airlines counter was super nice. Maybe he could sense the way I was battling tears. I'm not sure, but his tender, sweet voice kept me calm. After several minutes of hunting, he managed to find me a same-day ticket to LAX and told me I'd need to buy a ticket to Auckland when I got there. He warned me the wait in LA might take a while, especially if I couldn't catch one of today's flights. I told him I could handle it.

I passed over Dad's credit card and it was done. Just like that.

The phone in my pocket buzzes. I close my eyes, not wanting to check the message. It'll be Mack. I don't want to talk to him. I still can't believe he did it to me. My emotions are too fragile to entertain the idea that his desperate gaze was telling me he didn't do it. I can't think about it.

All I can do is leave.

I hope my note to the Fosters was enough.

My hurried scribble will give away my tenuous state. I'm grateful no one will be home until late afternoon. By the time they find my *thank you for having me* letter, I'll already be in the air. They'll no doubt call my parents immediately. I've already tried to counter the inevitable by making a quick, breezy call to my mum. I masked the real reason for my shaky voice by saying that I was badly homesick. She bought into it and told me to call her as soon as I reached LA. I have to keep her posted on my progress. She's got a big hug ready for me when I get home.

Home.

I don't want to go.

The tears I've been wrestling with sting so bad. I close my eyes and let them build behind my lids. My lips scrunch into an ugly line as I squeeze my temple. That cartoon was brutal...and the whole bloody school saw it.

Why can't I escape this?

I'm trying so hard to turn over a new leaf. Be someone likable.

The way I felt around Mack—that's who I want to be.

How could he shit all over it like that?

All those sweet words, the way his eyes would soften when he traced his finger down my cheek. The hours we spent talking and laughing together. The stories he told me. The way he let me in. I can't believe he could let it all go so easily. Unless it'd been fake right from the start. Some way to punish me for dissing him that first day.

The more I think about it, the more I'm convinced Layla put him up to it. Roxy and Michelle were probably involved too. Bitches.

I can't imagine Tori having anything to do with it, but she is dating a jock, so who the hell knows.

The cool, popular crowd sucks!

I should have known better.

People are the same the world over. The crowd I belong with is not one I want to be a part of.

So where does that leave me?

A piece of driftwood floating in an unforgiving ocean that's never going to let me forget.

I nearly killed Eloise Cochran…and I'm going to pay for it for the rest of my life.

29

EMPTY AND SILENT

MACK

I SAT ON THE FOSTERS' front step until my butt went numb. Kaija never showed.

I ditched school and spent the rest of the day driving to all the spots in Nelson where Kaija and I spent time together. She wasn't at any of them.

Pushing my front door open, I thump up the stairs to my room. A small hope that maybe she's on my bed makes me hustle, but when I burst through the door, all I find is an empty, silent room.

It's the mirror of my heart right now.

Empty.

Silent.

How could she assume it was me?

All the time we spent together and the hours we talked. She thought it was all bullshit. Some cruel con so I could demolish her so publicly.

I'm insulted…wounded…aching.

Snatching Dad's football off the window seat, I hug it to my chest and slump onto my bed. I wish he were here right now. He'd have something intelligent to say, something insightful that would help me solve this hideous mess.

I sigh and shake my head, my frown so deep it's giving me a headache. My chest hurts.

This probably seems dramatic, but how I feel right now is almost worse than when Dad died. We had time to adjust to his parting. It still sucked, and standing in the church for his funeral was the most numbing experience of my life. I didn't want to feel. I didn't want to think. I just stood with one arm around Layla and one around my mom. They were both whimpering and crying. I was the only one who managed to keep it together. I had to. I was the only *man* in the family, and I had to protect the ones left behind.

I may have only been thirteen, but I took that job seriously. When Martin came along a couple of years later, I backed off my mom, but Layla was still my responsibility and it kept me going.

And then Kaija arrived, and for the first time since that funeral I found something that I wanted for me. And it felt...liberating. Kaija was mine. I was hers. We had this happy bubble moment.

Now that bubble's popped.

And I don't know what to do.

"Hey." Layla's soft voice makes me jerk. I glance up to see her standing in my doorway. Her long hair is up in a high ponytail, the dark locks resting on her shoulder. The hoop earrings in each lobe are massive and they swing slightly when she lowers her bag to the floor and approaches me.

Her heeled boots sink into the carpet. I keep my eyes on them, unable to look at her face.

I wait until she's standing right beside me before quietly asking, "Was it you?"

As much as I wanted to reject the thought, I couldn't. It'd been festering all day. Logically, my sister was the only one who could have had any inkling of Kaija's past. I'd said something to her the night we drove to the mall, about Kaija understanding us. Layla isn't stupid. That one comment would have gotten her thinking.

Dammit! That made me responsible too! I should have kept my stupid mouth shut.

Layla bobs down in front of me so I'm forced to look at her face. Her nails are sharp as she squeezes my knee. "Of course it wasn't me."

Her voice is calm and soft. The fact that she's acting so gently probably means she can sense my raw torment. Her dark eyes swirl with a mix of emotions—they always do. I spot the slight insult at being accused, but I also see her worry for me. My sister may act like a self-absorbed brat sometimes, but she loves me...and I'm grateful for that.

"Those posters were cruel." She sighs and brushes a loose strand of hair off her cheek. "I may act like a bitch sometimes, but I'd never go that far."

"So, who would?"

"I don't know." Her earrings swing as she shakes her head. "I tried to ask around today, but the squad are all just as surprised as I am. We thought Kaija was a library geek. We had no idea she was capable of being that nasty. I thought she was just another Tori, trying to steal one of our guys."

I squeeze my eyes with a sharp huff. "Tori's not stealing Colt. Geez, Layla. They like each other. Can't you girls see that?"

"Yeah, we see it." Layla frowns. "How do you think it makes us feel? We put ourselves out there for you guys all the time. You party with us, make out with us, have sex with us...but you never fall in love with us. Tori is so quirky and weird, and she's scored one of the hottest guys on the team. And not just scored, they... He acts like he's in love with her." A sad frown wrinkles her perfect features as she takes a seat beside me. The mattress dips a little. She leans her head against my shoulder, her voice quivering a little. "Just like you act as though you're in love with Kaija."

"I am," I croak.

Layla pulls in a shaky breath. "How? She's... You've only known each other for such a short time."

"I don't know how." A smile crests my lips as I think about Kaija's eyes and the way they caught me that day in the gym. "She just... She captured me."

"And you captured her," Layla whispers.

"Not really." I blow out a breath. "If I had, she wouldn't be accusing me of doing something so cruel. She'd be answering my calls, she'd be letting me comfort her."

I bunch my mouth to stop my lips from shaking.

Layla sits back and rubs her hand across my shoulders. "We'll find out who did this, Mack. We'll make it right."

Running a hand through my hair, I dip my head and mutter, "Whoever did this is gonna have hell to pay."

Anger fires back through me, sharp and energetic. I hold onto it, liking the heat and intensity. It's easier to cope with than the simmering sadness that's trying to debilitate me.

I sit tall, trying to regain my strength, to put on the brave face I'm so good at showing. But it doesn't stop the whisper in the back of my mind.

Finding the culprit won't bring Kaija back to me...just like playing football never resurrected my dad.

30

H.O.M.E.

KAIJA

THE PLANE TOUCHES down in Auckland at 7.48 am on Wednesday morning. It's still Tuesday in Nelson, Idaho. I glance at my watch, wondering what Mack's doing. I can't remember what subject he's in on a Tuesday morning. If he's feeling anything like me, it won't matter. Concentrating on anything but the ache in my chest is basically impossible.

I hate that I'm thinking about him.

I want to burn him from my brain, but my heart just keeps wandering back. I miss him. I should want to curse him to a lifetime of torment. Why can't I do that?

The plane taxis to the terminal while I swallow down the idea that maybe, deep down, I know he's not responsible. You know what, I don't even care who is. It doesn't matter. It won't change anything. Mack and I could have never lasted. We were living in a fantasy, and rather than having a bittersweet ending we got the cruel, cut-your-heart-out version.

Pressing my head back against the seat, I rub my burning eyes. I haven't slept since waking on Monday morning. Trying to get comfortable on a plane is impossible. I managed to doze off a couple of times, but only for a few minutes. My body was still wired and buzzing from my impulsive travel arrangements. Once I reached LA, I had to transfer to the international terminal with all my bags. I lugged them up to the Air New Zealand counter and begged for a ticket. They had to put me on standby. I was gearing up for an overnighter in the airport when last minute they let me onto the 9.45 pm flight. Having fought tears all day, I finally let them loose. They came out of me in an ugly sob that made the poor Air New Zealand worker flinch away from me. He gave me a confused smile, then awkwardly patted my back and led me to the security check. I only just made the flight.

By the time I finally buckled my seatbelt, I was a total stress-bucket. It took me well after midnight before I even started to unwind. But I never slept.

That's all I want to do now.

Sleep.

Forget.

Pretend it never happened.

"Once again, folks, welcome to Auckland. Please wait until the seatbelt sign has been turned off before collecting your things and disembarking from the plane. We hope you had a pleasant flight. Air New Zealand thanks you for using our service."

How the flight attendant still sounds so chipper after a thirteen-hour flight, I'm not sure. I'd be ready to tear someone's head off. Flying sucks.

Tugging my carry-on bag out from under the seat in front of me, I hug it to my chest. Mum and Dad will be waiting for me at the arrivals gate. My lips wobble as I picture them. I'm bound to fall completely apart as soon as they wrap their arms around me. Dad's hugs are a sure-fire way to get me crying. He's so strong and protective…just like Mack.

You know you're past the 'Daddy's little girl' stage when you'd rather some other gorgeous guy hold you close while you snot and cry all over them. But here's the big difference—I trust my dad to never hurt me.

I can't feel the same about Mack anymore. That small voice inside just isn't loud enough. All I can do now is move forward and forget about my time at Nelson High.

————

Dad's arms are strong and secure around me. I let the tears fall. I'm past the ugly sob stage now and have reverted to the silent tears that are supposed to cleanse the pain.

They don't.

I'm still raw inside, like someone's ground my innards with a grater.

"This is such a surprise." Mum rubs the part of my back she can access.

I curl my fingers into Dad's T-shirt and murmur, "I missed you guys."

"We missed you too, Jellybean." Dad kisses the top of my head, then pulls back to grin down at me. "Come on, let's stop those tears, eh? Time to get you home."

I nod, slashing at my waterworks and forcing a quivering smile.

Mum's hazel eyes flicker with worry. In an attempt to ward off a long-winded interrogation, I wrap my arm around her waist and kiss her cheek. "It feels good to be home."

It doesn't, but I hope it sounds genuine enough.

The words bring a smile to her lips. "Good to have you back, baby girl."

Dad pushes the trolley for me and we head out to the vast parking lot. The vibrant buzz of comings and goings whirl around us. I watch people's faces—their smiles, both sad and excited—while Dad pays for the parking ticket.

Mum's still got her arm around me, no doubt keeping me close in fear that I might change my mind and leave her again. Her lips keep bunching, which is a sure sign she wants to ask me why I split so early.

"I'm glad I made this move," I lie. "It feels good to get back with enough time to prepare for school. The pressure was getting a bit too much for me and I just really needed to get home. I want a little break before school starts again."

"That's what I said to you." Mum nods. "Although, you probably could have told the Fosters in a nicer way. I don't think they appreciated the sudden departure."

"I know." I shrug. "It was selfish, but I just didn't want them to think I couldn't handle it and I knew if I tried to explain, they'd convince me to stay. I had to do what was right for me."

"True, my girl. I'm proud of you."

You shouldn't be.

That's what I want to say, but I don't. There's only a few people left in my life who still look at me like I'm not the spawn of Satan...or a murdering slut, as someone put it.

Anger fires through me—cold and blue. With such a hot, intensive flame, you'd think it would stick around, but the sick sadness roiling through me puts a swift end to the emotion. I'm too tired to feel angry. I think I'll just skip ahead to despair. Not sure I'll ever make it to acceptance though.

Why should I?

I don't deserve it.

That comic strip may have been horrible, but it's the truth. I did taunt someone to the point of wanting to kill herself. I tried to run, but even Nelson, Idaho wasn't far enough to get away from my transgressions.

"Your friends will be pleased to see you back." Dad grins as he slides the ticket into his pocket and starts pushing the trolley again. "They've been asking after you."

I'm sure they have.

I let go of Mum so she won't feel the tension in my muscles. She doesn't let on that she's noticed, just gives me one of those motherly grins and chides Dad, "Let her get some sleep and recover first. She can catch up with her friends when she doesn't feel so much like a zombie."

I'll try to stretch that excuse out. It takes at least a week or two to recover from jet lag, right? That'll bring me up to a week before school goes back.

School.

Going back.

Shit!

Mum tucks a lock of hair behind my ear before rubbing my shoulders and letting out a giddy chuckle. "It's so good to have you home."

I force a smile and nod, my mind reeling with images of my first day back at Macleans College.

As I follow Dad to our car, I realize that no matter how much I want to hide away, I can't. What I did will always be there...and no matter who I meet or where I end up, I can never erase the girl I once was. As much as I wanted Nelson High to redefine me, I still have no idea who I am, or who I'm meant to be. Hanging with the wrong crowd didn't work. My very first week I was drawn to Mack, and I couldn't resist him no matter how hard I tried.

So where does that leave me?

I'm returning to the one place I want to escape and I'm

somehow supposed to navigate it. I can't just fall back in with my old crowd. For one, I don't want to get caught up like that again and two, there's a strong chance there's no longer a place for me. I'm the girl the rumors are about. I'm the wicked one. The girl who took it too far.

If anything, I'll be returning with a target on my chest and no Mack to protect me.

He couldn't protect me at Nelson High, so why do I think he can do it here?

Because I want him to.

Because it's been less than 48 hours and I already ache for him.

Yes! Even in spite of the fact that he may have tried to ruin me, I miss him. I miss the way I felt when we were together. The way he smiled at me. How he made it so easy to talk to him. I miss the feel of his fingers skimming my cheekbone and his lips pressing against mine. The way his arms wrapped around me and held me close...

What we had was short and fleeting.

But man, it was precious. I'm never going to get it again.

All that awaits me now is a suck-fest year.

Tears burn my eyes and tingle in my nose. I can't let them show. I have to keep it in or Mum and Dad will want the whole story, in every ugly detail.

Dad opens the car door for me. I slip into the back seat and buckle up, preparing myself for home. A… **H**arrowing. **O**pen-slather. **M**acleans will kill me. **E**xperience.

31

WHO DUNNIT?

MACK

"COME ON, Sammy. I need you to do this for me." I have her boxed in against the outside gymnasium wall. The afternoon sun has crested over the building and huge shadows cover the out-of-sight space we're standing in. The snow hasn't yet melted in the shady spot, and it crunches under my boots as I lean in further and really get in her face.

Her sharp eyes narrow. "Back off. I'm not snooping around the Fosters' place, you asshole."

"You live right next door to them."

She shoves at my shoulders, but I don't budge. "I don't care where I live! I'm not breaking and entering so you can go accusing them of chasing your girlfriend off."

"There's got to be proof in their place. She was living in their spare room, maybe one of them stumbled across something. I've got to find some kind of evidence."

"No, man. You don't. It's been three weeks. You need to let this go."

I smack my hand into the wall above her head. "I'm not letting this go."

"Move out of my space or I'm gonna hurt you." Her thin eyebrows arch high.

I ignore her request, clenching my jaw and glaring at her. "Dana looks nervous every time I talk to her. She knows something."

"Everyone looks nervous when you talk to them! You're acting like the freaking Gestapo! You are aware that you are managing to alienate everyone in this school, right?"

"I'm just trying to find the truth!" I thunder.

"Don't be yelling in my face. Whether you like it or not, your little girlfriend did something bad. Now, I'm sorry that she was exposed the way she was, but if it were me, I would have owned that shit, apologized, and moved on. She ran. That was her choice, and you need to let her do that. Turning this place into Guantanamo is not helping you!"

"I'm after justice!"

"No! You're after revenge!"

This is so not going how it's supposed to. Sammy's always up for this kind of thing. Why the hell is she challenging me on my behavior? I'm not the one who plastered heinous cartoons all over the school. Did the culprit see Kaija's face, that wild, heart-wrenching agony in her eyes?

Did they feel bad for what they did?

I want them to know. I want them to look me in the eye and really understand how much pain they caused.

I can't reach her.

Kaija's not anywhere on the internet that I can find, and Anderson told me (under duress) that she hasn't responded to any of his emails. When I got shitty with him, he refused to give me her address and I'm back to nothing. No clue who dunnit, and no access to the one girl I'd do anything for.

I grit my teeth. "Just sneak in and have a look around, that's all I'm asking."

"I'm not doing that, Mack." Her firm, stubborn-ass voice sparks the powder keg in my belly.

"Damn it, Sammy! Help me out!" I roar in her face,

slapping the wall until I can feel the sting vibrating down my arm.

She brings my tantrum to a swift end by punching my in the stomach.

For a skinny chick, she's got some definite power going on there. I cough and slump over, holding my belly.

"Geez, Sam. Shit!" I wheeze. "Are you sure you're not a guy?"

She bends down and gets in my face. "Are you sure you're not a lunatic?"

I crumple to my knees, my jeans sinking into the snow and getting instantly wet. "I need to fix this," I finally croak.

Sammy sighs and crouches down beside me. My jacket rustles as her long fingers squeeze my shoulder. "Finding out the truth is not going to bring her back. Do you honestly think she cares? It wouldn't matter who did that to her. The second her secret was exposed, the damage was done."

I squeeze my eyes shut. "I need to prove it wasn't me."

"You know what? If she feels even half of what you feel for her, she won't believe you did it."

"She accused me…"

"She was terrified and humiliated. You were the only person she could unleash that on."

I let out a shaky sigh, then clench my jaw so hard my teeth start to hurt.

"This sucks, I know…but you need to pull yourself together. It's time to let go."

I sniff, finding it hard to swallow past the huge lump in my throat. "I miss her."

"Yeah, I really liked that chick. She was a little flaky, but the fact she managed to prank your ass gave her extra cred in my book."

I snicker. "The cupcakes were your idea, weren't they?"

Sammy's shoulder hitches with a shrug. "It was a team effort. The chili powder was her idea."

The deep sorrow I'm so used to living with feels heavier than usual. Ever since Kaija yelled in my face and took off, I've been living with a boulder inside of me. It's worse than when Dad died. It's like a second hole has been torn open inside of me, and the two have merged together into a cavernous space so big I don't know what to do with it.

"How do I let her go?"

"I don't know." Sammy purses her lips. "I guess you just get on with life and eventually the pain turns to…"

"A dull ache, that never quite leaves you." I rub my chest, thinking of Dad and how many times I've thrown a football in his name, trying to squash that lingering pain.

"Why'd she make you so happy?"

The question surprises me for some reason. I turn to find Sammy's blue eyes studying me.

"She…" I grin. "She challenged me. She made me think. Dream. Feel…things I never had before. I really liked it."

Sammy's smile grows, pushing her narrow face wide. "Glad it wasn't just about her smoking-hot bod."

"Yeah, well, there was that too."

We share a laugh, but it's fleeting.

"So those dreams…those challenges." Sammy tips her head. "The way she made you think. Maybe that's what you should be focusing on right now."

I want to argue that I can't do any of that stuff without her, but that would be a lie. As much as I hate to admit it, Sammy's right. Trying to find this asshole is killing me, and I'm not getting any closer to winning Kaija back. I need to sort out my shit. Get my head straight.

Maybe if I start living the life I want, instead of the one

everyone expects me to, I can figure out how to fill this space inside of me. Then, if I'm really lucky, when I do eventually find Kaija, I'll be presenting her with a whole person and not just Bob Mahoney's broken son.

32

KEEP WALKING FORWARD

KAIJA

MY LEGS ARE TREMBLING. This is so stupidly insane. This will be my fifth year at Macleans College, but I'm walking through the main entrance like it's my first.

Eyes are on me.

I can feel them as I brush past people.

I haven't spoken to any of them since I left for the States. The night of my final exam, I flew out—my futile attempt at escape.

"Hey, Green Eyes." My muscles tense at the sound of Hanson's voice behind me.

My insides used to bubble and whizz at that sound.

Now they burn…and not the good burn, but the sick, vile one that makes you want to throw up.

His long fingers skim down my arm.

I flick him off me and move to the side.

The body I used to lust after appears beside me. He's leaning down, getting in my space. "I tried calling you."

"I know." I scratch the side of my nose and look away.

"So did Anna."

"Yep." I nod.

He purses his lips, making an irritating little whistling sound while brushing the floppy, light-brown locks off his forehead. "Why the cold shoulder?"

"Really?" My eyes snap to his. "You expect me to be all chummy after the shit you wrote about me? You and Anna had a field day."

"It's just Facebook."

"Facebook lasts forever. Every picture you post and word you write. They own that."

His jaw works to the side as he looks over my shoulder and tries to pretend like he hasn't done anything wrong.

"We were just joshing."

"Yeah, well, your comedy routine needs some major work."

He snickers, then brushes the back of his finger across my cheek. I slap his hand away and glare at him. He rolls his eyes and I take my leave. Unfortunately, he doesn't pick up on my very unsubtle hints and runs to catch up with me.

"How was the States?"

"I don't want to talk to you."

He pulls me to a stop, his grip firm and unrelenting. "So, this is how it's going to be? You try to kill someone and then you just run away and stonewall your friends?"

I fire him an incredulous look. "I didn't try to…" I catch myself when I spot the smirk on this face. He's goading me. The glint in his eye makes me want to slap him. But I can't draw attention to myself. I'm already a murdering slut; I don't want to add douchebag basher to my list.

I swallow and will my erratic heart to find a rhythm that doesn't make me want to pass out.

"I was in hell, and the first thing you did was slather my mistake all over the internet. You even said I supplied the pills. What the f—" I let out a breath, hating the way my voice is shaking. "I don't want to be that person anymore. I don't need you. I don't want you in my life."

"You breaking up with me?"

"What are you on?" I fling my arms wide. "I dumped you the day you jumped on Anna's little bandwagon. You were my boyfriend. I came to you for help, protection, and you treated my nightmare like some joke! You used it as a weapon against me so you would come off looking squeaky clean. And you know the worst part? I did most of that stuff to Eloise to try to impress you. I drove her to suicide to score with you." I let out a derisive sound that hopefully gives away my utter disgust and repulsion. "Worst mistake of my life."

His expression darkens, his handsome face turning an ugly shade of red. "Well, don't hold back or anything."

"You're scum." I poke my finger into his chest. "Don't talk to me again."

He snickers. "Welcome back to school, bitch."

"Screw you." I flip him off.

"This is going to be the worst year of your life."

"You don't have to tell me that." He has no idea. Losing him was a drop in the bucket compared to losing Mack. I storm away, ignoring the whispers and stares happening around me. My skin is crawling from standing so close to that asshole. It felt good to say it to him straight, but it just makes me miss Mack. I've been hiding away in my room since returning home. Of course my first social interaction with a peer had to be with Hanson Bloody Whitelock.

He's right about one thing—this year is going to suck.

But not because of the shitstorm I'm walking back into.

It's going to be the worst year ever because it doesn't include Mack...and I don't know what transpired to bring my time in Nelson to such a brutal end, but I do know that I haven't stopped dreaming about Mack since I left. Not one day goes by without him whistling through my mind.

I miss him.

I miss his smile, his eyes...his arms.

Hustling through the quad, I sense a penetrating gaze trying to bore a hole through my head. I turn and see Anna. Her glare could melt steel. I shuffle away from it, swiveling so all she can see is the back of my head as I run away from her.

It's weird that facing Hanson was easier than chatting to the girl I would have sworn was my best friend. She's pissed with me because I took off to America and gave her the silent treatment. She's going to make me pay for mistreating her. Ironic, right?

Typical that she expects me to arrive back at school and

pretend like nothing went down. She's delusional. Just like I used to be. For a while there, nothing could touch me. But I know better now. I've been wiped out by tragedy…and now by love.

I've got nothing left, and all I can do is keep walking forward.

33

THE RAW TRUTH

MACK

MY PALMS ARE SWEATING as I walk into the gymnasium for our Monday morning assembly. Colt and I have been getting a lot of looks this morning.

Why? Because it's National Signing Day. The day we both scrawl our names on a letter of intent and bind ourselves to the university we will play football at for at least the next year.

Thanks to a little help from Tori, which I'm not actually supposed to know about, Colt kept up his grades and was able to play for the entire season. The day after we won the division championship, he got a verbal offer from the Broncos, including a full scholarship.

And today it becomes official. He's taking another step towards his dream of playing pro ball.

Me, I'm a different story.

Thoughts of my mom send a spiral of nerves whirling through my ribcage. The Sahara Desert has moved into my respiratory system and is making it damn near impossible to breathe. I haul in some air, but it feels stale and dry. My chest hurts. My head is pounding.

But I gotta do this.

If I can tell the school then maybe it'll give me the courage to tell the woman with the highest expectations of all.

Everyone nestles into their seats around the gymnasium...except for Colt, me, and a few other athletes who have scored athletic scholarships around the country. It's a big day for us. A day to be proud.

"Okay, settle down everyone," Principal Matthis speaks into the microphone.

The loud chatter simmers down to a hushed murmur. I stare into the stands and notice Layla sitting with her girls. She smiles at me, her pride obvious. I give her a closed-mouth grin and look away. What's she going to think?

My eyes keep trailing across the audience as Principal Matthis goes on about how proud the faculty is of these high-achieving students. Everyone has worked hard, blah, blah, blah.

The last time I was front and center like this was after we won the championship. The school gave us rousing applause as we stood on the stage, cocky as hell while we reveled in the glory of beating the Bears. I'd been grinning from ear to ear, my eyes honed in on Kaija. She'd rolled her eyes at me and kept her gaze on the floor, but I'd kept watching her anyway.

I miss her.

"...a few words from our Raider's captain, Mack Mahoney." Principal Matthis points at me and I force that cheesy grin everyone seems to love.

My legs are kind of shaky as I step forward and take the mic. The last time I spoke into this thing, I was hyping everyone up for the big game. I doubt my speech today will have the same effect.

"Hey, guys."

My simple greeting receives a wolf whistle from the back row, which makes the assembly erupt with laughter. I smile and wait for it to pass.

Swallowing down the sand in my throat, I grip the microphone and look around the room. The speech I spent last night composing sticks to the sides of my brain like gum. All I can feel is an intense exhaustion and weariness. My plan to go on about making choices and trying to inspire the student body flies out the window. All I've got left is the raw truth.

"So, uh, thank you, Mr. Matthis, for letting me speak today." The principal nods at me, his smile broad and filled with pride. I look away from him and try to find someone to focus on. I spot Finn and Tyler, their eyebrows both raised with expectation. Nah, that won't do. I shift my gaze away from them and find Layla. Her nose wrinkles as she grins at me and spins her hand for me to get talking. I give her a tender smile. "I know you're probably expecting some kind of rousing speech about the awesomeness of football and how incredibly lucky I feel to be in this position. I've loved the game since I was a kid…and I always will."

Glancing at the gym floor, I squeak my sneaker over the polished surface.

"But then I discovered something I love more." I look up. "I met someone who showed me that life is more than just playing the game. She made me realize that my future is my own and I'm the only person responsible for living the life I want." I shake my head with a sad smile. "You know, people accused her of being a liar, but I've never met a more honest person. They slammed her for trying to make a fresh start, for trying to figure out who she wants to be. They made her feel bad for moving on from a past she wants to forget." My voice rises with fervor and I have to press my lips together to stop myself from shouting. "Kaija Bennett made a mistake, and she's going to have to live with that. She doesn't need people reminding her. Why do you think she left New Zealand and came all the way here? She was after a new beginning…a way to try and redeem herself…to redefine who she was, so she never fell into the trap of hurting someone again. And what did she get for that? Crucified."

A hush falls over the assembly. The quiet murmurs are cut off at the knees, and all I can hear now is the awkward shifting of butts on bleachers. I scan the crowd for guilty faces, but there's too many people around me.

I let out a resigned sigh and keep going. "Nelson High is a great school, but we fail when it comes to accepting each other. The expectations in this place are insane and stupid. Cool, jock, popular, pretty, nerd, weirdo. Who gives a shit? If I want to be in love with someone who's got a past then that's my prerogative. None of us have any right to judge and point fingers. And I just want to take a minute to apologize for the way I've been acting these past few weeks. I've been scouring this school trying to find out who was responsible for outing Kaija. I got nothing. Someone here is an expert liar. I don't know who you are, and as much as I want to find you and beat the living shit out of you…I'm not going to do it. At the end of the day, it won't bring her back to me." I croak out the last few words.

Layla's staring at me with tears in her eyes. I wonder if she knows where I'm going with this…or maybe she's just thinking about losing the ones we love.

An image of Dad smiling up at me from the bed takes over, his skin pale and his cheeks sunken in. His eyes still glowed though. Even in those final days, he always knew how to inspire me. He always had the right words.

I sniff, hoping some of his awesomeness has rubbed off. "It's no secret to any teenager in the world that life is sometimes shit."

Principal Matthis straightens, his thin eyebrows dipping together. That's the third time I've sworn, and I probably won't get away with a fourth. I ignore his scowl and press on.

"It's hard to figure out who you want to be and where you want to go in life. Since my dad died, I've been working my butt off trying to be the son, the brother, the friend, the player…the captain that people want me to be. I've been doing anything I could to fill that gap in my chest. I thought if I just worked hard enough, if I just trained that little bit more, then maybe that empty feeling would go away." I press my fist into my chest and shake my head. "It never did.

Dad's not coming back, no matter what I do. And I'm tired of this fight."

The sand in my chest turns to liquid mush, making it hard to swallow. My eyes start burning. I clench my jaw and sniff in a short breath. "So that's why I won't be signing with the Boise State Broncos today."

It's like the air's been sucked from the room. Out of the corner of my eye, I see Tyler flinch. I hear my sister gasp and then a flurry of conversation whips around the gymnasium.

"Okay, quiet down. Quiet down, everybody!" Principal Matthis tries to yell over the noise, but it's pointless.

I press the mic to my lips and clear my throat. A hush settles over the student body. I'm now facing a sea of gaping faces.

"I know this is hard for you guys to understand. But I hope that my decision will encourage you to think about what *you* want. Don't live the life your parents and peers expect you to. Don't be afraid to say how you feel, to apologize, to be honest with your friends. Everyone has their quirks..." I find Tori in the crowd and wink at her. She grins back at me. "Everyone has their secrets, and that should be okay. Don't be scared to be who you are, to change what you need to in order to get the things you want. Figure out what you love and then chase that dream. That's what I'm gonna do."

I pass the mic back to Principal Matthis before my voice cracks. I get no applause for my speech. The golden boy of Nelson High has just told everyone he's not playing anymore. The stunned silence is near deafening. I don't know what the repercussions will be, but I've been true to myself and that's all I can do for now.

I glance over my shoulder and catch Colt's gaze. He's not gaping at me like I expected. Instead, his lips pull into a sad, yet accepting grin. He holds out his fist. I tap my knuckles against his and the weight of my big decision finally lifts off my shoulders.

34

MAIL

KAIJA

MY FEET scuff the ground as I walk home from school. I've been back at Macleans College for nearly two months now and it's been horrible. I'm trying to put on a brave face at home, but I'm sure Mum's worried. I've lost my appetite, my energy...even my smile. I knew going back would be bad and, as predicted, I am most definitely in no man's land.

Hanson promised me the worst year of my life and he's delivering. Anna's taken my place as the cool bitch of the school, and I think she's reveling in the position. They both take great delight in taunting me the way I used to taunt Eloise. I don't say anything. I never respond. I'm fully deserving of this treatment.

People at school act like I have leprosy. It's probably

self-preservation, so I really don't blame them. I nibble my lunch alone on the edge of the field and I sit by myself in every single class. Eloise hasn't come back, which isn't really helping my cause. Rumors continue to circulate as people try to decide why she hasn't returned.

She's homeschooling with her mum and apparently not liking it very much. My mother has been trying to get me to visit her for weeks, but I can't bring myself to look her in the eye. They'll tell me too much, give away just how badly I hurt her.

Now that I'm getting a taste of my own medicine, I really understand what she went through.

It makes me hate myself just a little bit more.

I stop at my letterbox and clear the mail before shuffling up the front path. As usual, the key sticks in the lock. I jiggle it and, with a grunt, kick the bottom corner until the door pops open. Sliding the bag off my shoulder, I dump it next to the shoe rack then start thumbing through the mail. My forehead wrinkles when I see my name scrawled on a small, padded envelope.

It's from the Fosters.

Anderson tried to reach me a few times after I left, but I refused to take his calls and I haven't cleared my email once since returning from the States. I only ever use my computer for schoolwork now. Social media is nothing but a curse. Sure, I feel completely out of the loop, but it's not just any old loop—it's a burning ring of fire, and I'm right in the center of it.

Dropping the rest of the mail on the table, I tuck the package under my arm and head upstairs to my room. I have no idea what's inside. It feels like a lipstick tube or something. Surely they wouldn't waste money posting me the lip-gloss I left behind.

I check the date stamp—February 24. It's taken nearly two weeks to reach me. My curiosity is in overdrive as I close my bedroom door and shuffle to my bed. Slumping down on my rumpled covers, I rip the package open and shake it until a flash drive plops out. Unfolding the note, I read Anderson's handwriting....

I've been trying to decide whether or not to send this to you. Part of me never wants you to see it, but Tori went off on me the other day when I admitted I had a recording. She called me a selfish prick before storming off.

I grin, imagining her wild curls bouncing as she marched her little body off in a huff.

Tori's not usually one for insults. It shocked the hell out of me...

but maybe she's right. You do deserve to see this. I would have emailed it to you, but you don't seem to be replying to my messages. This was the only move I had left. I hope you're doing okay, and I'm sorry for everything that went down.

If you ever get over it, I'd love to hear from you.

Andy

I pick up the flash drive, running my thumb over the smooth plastic as I make my way to the computer. Slotting it into the side, I drum my fingers on my desk as nerves rattle my system. It's obviously important if he's gone to the trouble of posting it to me.

My computer hums as I double-click the icon and select the mp4 file inside. My VLC player takes a minute to load, and then Mack appears on my screen. He's standing in the middle of a crowded gymnasium, holding a microphone. My breath hitches as I gaze at his frozen image. He's still gorgeous. I brush the screen with my finger, tracing the line of his jaw. The ache inside hasn't shrunk or grown, it's just been a constant feeling in the middle of my chest. I dream about him all the time.

Holding my breath, I hover my finger over the mousepad. One click and I'll get a decent dose of the guy I don't want to love anymore. Do I close the lid and walk away? Will hearing his voice make me feel worse, or will it work like an addictive balm?

The air whooshes out of my mouth, my chest deflating as I tap the mouse pad and his image comes to life.

"…people accused her of being a liar," Mack said.

I don't know how his speech started or why he was talking to the school in the first place, but whatever he said obviously compelled Anderson to pull out his phone and press Record.

My eyes glisten as I listen to Mack defending me, speaking so highly of me…acting as though he loved me. He had no idea I'd one day be watching him say all this stuff. Did that mean… Did that mean he meant it? The inkling that he wasn't to blame flares up inside me. It's like a whoosh of fresh air blasting through my body.

"…won't be signing with the Boise State Broncos today."

Surprised laughter punches out of me. He did it.

I blink at the tears on my lashes, letting them crest down my cheeks. Mack's still talking…about his dad. His voice is kind of husky now, made deep with emotion. I want to reach into the computer screen and hug him.

He's going to pursue *his* dream. I love his words about not being afraid...about apologizing. Was he thinking of me when he said them? On some supernatural level, did he know just how badly I needed to hear them?

Mack passes the mic to Principal Matthis and the video stops. I watch it again...and again...and again, until I have Mack's speech memorized. It must have taken so much courage for him to say that to the entire school. I can only imagine what it took to tell his mother.

I want to call him. To hear his voice and check that he's okay...but there's something else I have to do first. Snatching my handbag off the back of the chair, I grab my wallet and shades, not even bothering to change out of my uniform before running for the door.

———

Eloise's front door is pale blue. It looks stupid against the rest of the black, stained house, but it's always been her favorite color. If I remember her parents, they'll be doing everything in their power to make things perfect for Eloise. Maybe they hold themselves responsible for what happened. I did throw out that note, so they were no doubt mystified by their daughter's sudden suicide attempt.

My insides feel like grated onion—raw and weeping.

It's making my eyes burn and my nose tingle. Walking has never been so difficult.

"If Mack can lay his shit bare, then so can you. Keep walking," I boss myself.

Forcing my feet up the path, I come to a stop outside that blue door and hold my breath. Who would have thought that knocking on a front door could be the hardest thing in the world?

I rap three times, then step back and rub my knuckles. I hope someone answers quickly, because I don't have the courage to knock again.

The door swings open to reveal Mrs. Cochran. Her narrow head pings back on her long neck, her hazel eyes tightening at the corners while she assesses me.

"Hello, Kaija."

"Hi, Mrs. C. How's it going?"

She nods and gives me a fleeting smile.

"What can I do for you, hun?" Her body shifts into the open space, the small movement showing off her protective streak.

I swallow. "I need to see Eloise...if she's willing to talk to me."

"It's taken you a while."

"I've…b-been away."

"Your mother said you got back in January." Mrs. Cochran folds her arms, tipping her head with a skeptical frown.

"I, um…" Saying I've been busy at school isn't going to cut it. I mean, I *have* been busy, but that's only because I'm trying to make up for such poor exam results last year.

"What's suddenly brought you here today?"

My face bunches as an overpowering swell of tears takes hold of me. I blink and purse my lips, trying to keep it together.

Mrs. Cochran doesn't move. Her face remains neutral, giving me nothing. I have no idea what's come out in Eloise's counseling sessions, but from the hard set of Mrs. Cochran's jaw, I imagine my name's been brought up.

"Um," my voice quakes. "I-I need to apologize for being such a bad friend. It's been eating me alive for months, and I've…" I shake my head, losing my mental capacity for words. "Fear," I blurt. "It's just been plain old fear that's stopped me."

Mrs. Cochran looks to the top step, uncrossing her arms and gripping the door like she needs it for support. "I can imagine finding her on your bed like that must have had a huge impact on you."

"Scared the shit out of me."

The woman's lips twitch.

"Look, I know I have no right to see your daughter. I hurt her. I was cruel, and she should never have to see me again. I can just tell you what I came to say and then leave. I don't want to cause her any more pain or distress. I guess I just need her to know how sorry I am and that her...her suffering wasn't in vain. It's changed me. And this might sound warped, but I want to thank her for that."

The door pulls open a little wider and there she is.

Eloise stares down at me, those eyes I was so afraid to look at large and filled with surprise.

I lift my hand and try to wave, and all the love I used to have for her bubbles to the surface. Memories of how solid we were before she left for Myanmar taunt me until I let out a whimper and cover my mouth. My shoulders shake as I break down right on their front path and start blubbering.

"I'm sorry. I'm so, so sorry."

Crumpling to my knees, I bend over myself and go for it. The ugly sounds coming out of me are probably scaring off the dogs in the street, but I can't stop them.

Tears and snot paint my face as my stomach jerks and hiccups.

The door creaks above me and I sense a shuffling of feet, and then someone's arm is around me, rubbing my back and telling me it's alright.

I glance up and spot Eloise's sweet smile. My face bunches with confusion and she grins at me. "Come on, you. Get your sorry arse up and come inside. We've got some talking to do."

———

We talk until after midnight.

She tells me everything she went through leading up to her suicide attempt. Counseling's helped her unearth that the suicide wasn't just about me. She was feeling the pressure from school, needing to be perfect because she couldn't control the other areas in her life. She became obsessed with scoring perfect grades, being the perfect daughter, and when she couldn't do it, it ate her alive. Finally, she came to a point where the only thing she could control was whether or not to live or die.

"The counselor said that maybe deep down, my attempt was more of a cry for help. I just needed someone to hear me and see how desperate I was feeling. I didn't know how to talk about everything going on inside of me. I felt so out of control. Putting on a brave face all the time is exhausting. She's helping me see that I can make choices to reduce the pressure. I don't have to pretend anymore, because I *do* have control. I have a voice...and I can choose to use it whenever I want to. I am the only person who owns my destiny." Her voice comes out with a force I've never heard in her before.

"That's awesome, Elly."

She tucks her feet beneath her and hugs the pillow a little tighter to her chest. "I'm sorry I did it in your room."

My eyes round. *She's apologizing to me?*

"It's..." I shake my head. "It's...okay."

"No, I..." She shrugs and looks kind of pained. I scramble for a way to change the subject. The only person who should be apologizing is me. I'm not sure how many more ways I can do it, but I'll think of some.

"My counselor wonders if I attempted it in your room not to punish you but because you were the only person I used to tell everything to." Her head bobs and she looks to the ceiling. "And you know, I think she might be right. You were always my safe place, Kai. I went to you about everything and when you weren't there anymore, I felt completely lost. And then you were mean to me and..."

Her voice drops away and it's like a spear through my heart.

On impulse, I move down the bed and wrap my arms around her. "I swear I'll never do that to you again. I'm glad you were in my room, because it was the wake-up call I needed. You were my best friend, and seeing you that way was pure agony. I thought you were dead. I was scared I'd lost you. I know I acted like a first-class bitch, but you've been my girl for life…and I don't want that to change." I squeak out the last few words before pulling back and attempting a smile.

Tears are swamping my eyes again. I've never cried this much before, not even the nights I mourned over losing Mack. Right now, my eyes are aching and my head is thumping, the pressure so tight I wonder if my brain's going to start oozing out my ears. There's no way I can handle school tomorrow. All I want to do is hang out with Eloise and make up for the time we lost.

"You ever coming back to school?"

Eloise shrugs. "I hope so. Homeschooling with my mum is…painful."

"Yeah, well, school's not much better." I sigh.

"Really?" Eloise's head tips to the side.

"You'll be pleased to know that I'm getting a taste of my own medicine. I deserve it. It's not easy, but it's good for me. At least I know the type of people I want to hang out with now."

My mind flies to Mack and I dip my head before I can give away how much I'm hurting. This is about making amends with Eloise, not lamenting my broken heart.

Her hand rubs up and down my arm. "Well, maybe I'll think about coming back. We can be outcasts together."

I snicker. "I think I could handle that."

Eloise's face lifts with a grin that makes her eyes sparkle. "Me too."

35

LOVE DOESN'T COME EASY

MACK

MOM'S barely spoken to me since I made my big announcement at school. Layla's been really quiet too. Something's up with her, but the more I ask, the more she pulls away from me. The house is dead at the moment; even Martin's stopped whistling. It's kind of like living in a mausoleum, and I'm not sure how much more I can take.

My big speech rocked the school. Whispers followed me for about three weeks before they finally died down. I had every look, from respected awe to bewilderment to disdain.

The school's social structure certainly showed its true colors. Some of the guys on the team who had been looking up to me since starting Nelson High stopped talking to me, while others didn't know how to act around me. Luckily for me, Colt was on my side. Plus Finn always had my back, and Tyler was a loyal puppy. Whether he agreed with me or not, I still wasn't sure. But he was standing up for me around every corner.

My future is now wide open and, as intimidating as that feels, it's also liberating. I don't know which path to take. I've gone from one to a dozen. There are so many roads I could go down. I've always been inter-ested in the sciences, and becoming a sports doctor like Kaija's older brother sounds really interesting, but then business studies fascinate me too. Numbers have always come easy, and pursuing a career in finance sounds intriguing. I'm just going to have to enroll in a college somewhere and figure it out. But which one?

My insides kick every time I ask myself that question, because there's only one thing I know for certain...only one path that's tugging on my heart.

The problem is, I'm not sure how to take it.

I haven't spoken to Kaija since she accused me of pulling the long con. But today, after school, when we were hanging out at Briggs Burgerhouse, Tori approached our table with some exciting news. Colt shot from his seat and plucked her off the ground. She wrapped her short little legs around his waist and they made out right there in the middle of the restaurant.

Watching them together hurt so bad. I want that again. I *need* it.

I seriously have to go get my girl.

Busting in the front door, I rush up to my room and check my email, like I do every single day. There's no message from Kaija. I don't know what to expect, really —that she'll suddenly forgive me? It's been weeks. Would she still be mad if I just turned up on her doorstep? Or will that connection we have be enough? One look changed everything for me. Could I somehow make that happen again?

The rap of knuckles on wood makes me spin. I sit straight and prepare myself as Mom wanders into the room. With a heavy sigh, she sinks down onto the end of my bed.

"I hate this day. Every year, it hurts." A soft tremor runs through her voice.

I try to smile at her. "Yeah, I know."

"Do you think it always will?"

"Maybe." I shrug. "But I'm guessing Dad would want you to remember him with a smile on his birthday."

"That's what Martin said." She grins. "He told me I should make a cake or take you kids out to dinner, turn this day into a celebration instead." Her shoulders slump. "But I just don't think I have it in me."

"I can't imagine Layla going for it either."

Mom lets out a derisive laugh. "No. Your sister's got a ways to go yet."

We both go quiet. I don't know what Mom's thinking about but right now, I'm remembering Dad's last birthday. He was undergoing chemo, but still wanted a big party. People crowded into our house, trying to ignore the stench of impending death…trying to act as though Dad would recover and things would go back to normal. Dad had covered his bald head with fake tattoos and Layla spent most of the party suctioned to him. I'd hung back, not wanting to get too close, or make myself too vulnerable. Even at twelve, I could sense what was coming, and I was already making myself battle-ready.

"I fell in love with your father the very first day I met him. You look just like him, you know." Her eyes shimmer as she smiles at me. "He was playing football. It wasn't a Raiders game or anything; they were just messing around after practice. He collected the ball off the snap, then ran back and was about to launch it down the field when I caught his eye. We both just stood there staring at each other, and the rest of the world disappeared…until he got sacked by Uncle Wade."

Mom's back there right now. I can tell by the glassy

look on her face and the dreamy lilt in her voice. She chuckles and shakes her head.

"He loved the game so much…" She tips her head. "But I think he loved me more." She sniffs, her eyes hitting me with an unexpected strength. "When you told me you weren't signing that letter of intent, I was heartbroken, because I felt like I was losing your dad all over again. Everything you've done has emulated him and now you're breaking away. I don't know what to do with that. I thought playing made you feel close to him."

"It does." I nod. "Which is why I'll always be up for a casual game of touch or messing around with the guys. But Mom, following in his footsteps won't bring him back. I have to accept the fact that Dad's gone, and I can't be responsible for keeping his memory alive. I've got to walk my own path."

Mom's face bunches as she tries to smile and nod.

"I'm sorry it hasn't worked out the way you wanted," I murmur.

Mom won't look at me as she shakes her head and smoothes down her skirt. "It's okay, Mack. You are just like your father. You love football…but you love her more."

My lips part.

"I'm not blind, honey. You haven't been the same since she left. I don't know everything that happened or why she's suddenly gone, but…" She looks up at me with a tender smile. "She must be something real special."

"She is," I croak. "But, uh…" I shake my head. "I'm not just doing this for her."

"Good." Mom smiles.

"Besides, I don't know if she wants me. I can't reach her and, um…" I clear my throat. "What do I do? Mom, what do I do?"

She gets off the bed and walks across to me, crouching at my feet and resting her hand on my tightly threaded fingers. "Getting together with your father was the easiest thing in the world. When I lost him, I thought I'd never feel joy again. But then within a couple of years, Martin came along."

My stomach clenches, but I force myself not to react.

"I know you kids don't love him, but he fought for me and I am so grateful. Love doesn't always come easy, Mack. But the relationships you have to work for, they are precious… They're worth it. Don't let her fears, or yours, stop you from having something beautiful. Be romantic. Sweep her off her feet. Do something that proves how much you care about her. She'll have no choice but to stop and listen then."

Mom's face starts glowing, and I hope to God she doesn't launch into details of how Martin finally got her attention. I distract her with one of my megawatt smiles, then wrap my arms around her.

"Love you, Mom."

"Oh, sweetie. I love you too." She grips me tight, her last-ditch effort to hang onto me.

She doesn't know it, but I'm already gone.

I know what I have to do now, and I hope like heck my mom will help me pull it off.

36

CAN I HAVE YOUR ATTENTION, PLEASE?

KAIJA

I HAVEN'T FOUND the courage to email Mack yet. I don't know what to say to him. I've typed so many emails that are now sitting in my trash folder, unsent. I feel kind of mean considering the beauty of his speech. The longer I leave it, the bigger the gap between us grows. He's probably already getting over me.

I showed the speech to Eloise on the weekend and she's convinced it's an invitation for me to initiate contact...but he didn't even know Anderson was recording it! Eloise rolled her eyes at me. I think she was enjoying listening to someone else's problems instead of talking about her own for a change.

She started school last week. Her mum dropped us off and we walked down the stairs side-by-side, into the big quad area. We didn't make eye contact with anyone, just stuck together like glue until we were forced to go our separate ways when the bell rang. I've been keeping a really close eye on her this week. Anna and her crew of bitches are no doubt brewing something, but I'll scratch faces if I have to. No one's getting near Eloise this time.

It feels good to fight for someone. To be on the right side for a change.

As usual my mind goes to Mack and how he fought for me…stood up against his whole school…and I still can't find the words to thank him. I don't know why I'm making such a big deal of this.

Maybe it's because I'm scared that if I connect with him again, I'll never get over him. He may not be going to Boise State anymore, but none of those college apps on his desk were for Auckland University. We can't make this work. It's too hard.

I hate that logic hurts. It should be making me feel better, not worse.

Hitching my bag onto my shoulder, I tug on my stupid blue shirt. This uniform is so ugly. I can't wait for this wretched year to be over! It's currently March and school doesn't finish until early December. Oh, man, I hope I can do it!

I scan the main quad for Eloise but she's not there. We

usually walk to school together, but she had a counseling session this morning and isn't getting here until morning break. Well, it's morning break and she's still not here.

I spot Anna and Hanson smirking at me from bench seats near the graphic design rooms. It's the cool kids' new hangout spot, and it's a pain in the ass because everyone has to pass there to get to the tuck shop or down to the field. It's the central walkway and they sit on the seats like a row of seagulls, mocking and sneering as students walk past.

I turn my back on their smug smiles, trying to be unaffected by the fact that I'm standing like a lone loser. I don't give a shit. I only have eight and a half months of this crap to go. Clenching my jaw, I hold in my sigh and focus on the glimmer of crystal water I can see in the distance. Macleans backs onto Eastern Beach, and the view from the fields is absolutely stunning. I stride over to the edge of the quad for a better look. I may as well head down to the field and watch the guys play rugby.

I'm just moving that way when a screeching Eloise makes me jerk and spin to face her.

"Kaija!" She runs down the stairs so fast she nearly loses her balance. The seagulls scoff and squawk from their perch. Eloise ignores them and jumps down the last few steps, turning her trip into a skip.

Her blue skirt twists askew as she races over to me with bright eyes.

I capture her hands when she reaches me. "Far out, how good was your counseling session this morning?"

She giggles and shakes her head. Her hands are quivering as she shakes mine.

"There is a super-hot guy..." She puffs then swallows, trying to catch her breath. "He's at the front office." She points behind her. "He's asking for you."

My head jerks back. "What?"

"You know the best part?"

I tip my head, still trying to process what she's telling me. What guy?

"I recognize him...from this video I saw on the weekend."

My breath hitches. My mind fuzzes, buzzes...suddenly stops working. "He... Is it...?"

"Yes!" Eloise squeals, then jumps on her toes.

I can't move. I don't know what's wrong with me. I should be running for that office, but I'm kind of in shock right now. My heart doesn't know what to do with itself.

It can't be Mack.

He wouldn't…

I look up.

And there he is…standing at the top of the stairs, gazing down at me. For a second, I relive our first moment—that look we shared. We're doing it again. Staring at each other like it's the only thing we were made to do.

My stomach does this little flippy thing, then nestles down nice and slow on a wistful sigh that tells me everything is going to be okay now. My heart should be racing but it's not. It's calm and warm, and knows just what to do.

A smile stretches my mouth wide as I step around my jumping friend and walk towards Mack.

He looks tired. His clothes are crumpled and his hair's all mussed, but nothing can take away from that grin on his face. Hot damn. He lopes down the stairs. He's in jeans, a T-shirt and his letterman jacket. He couldn't look more American if he tried. I love that about him.

Everyone in the quad is picking up on this epic moment. I can feel eyes on us from every bench seat, window, and pathway. I can sense their whispers. "Who's that guy?"

I don't care what they're saying. Nothing can stop me from wrapping my arms around his neck the second he's within reach. With a husky chuckle, he picks me up off the ground and holds me close. My legs wind around his waist, twisting at the ankles while I squeeze the life out of him. His arms encase me, his broad hands splaying over my back as he holds me securely.

What we have isn't a lie.

There's no con. No prank.

Just raw, unchecked emotion made up of all the good things life has to offer.

"You're here." My voice quivers.

"I didn't know how else to get your attention."

I squeeze a little tighter, tears brimming on my lashes as I murmur, "I love you."

He sighs and shifts his hands beneath my thighs so he can lean back and look at me with a tender smile. "You don't know how badly I needed to hear that."

"You don't know badly I needed to see you here." I sniff and slash my tears away. "You came all the way to New Zealand…just to get my attention."

He shrugs. "I needed to show you how big the feels were."

I grin and bite my lip before burying my hands in his luscious locks and bending forward to kiss him. He tastes just the same, his warm lips filling me with that intoxicating mixture of electricity and comfort. His arms grip me tighter while his tongue dives into my mouth.

The bell tries to pull us apart, letting out a shrill ring that sends a wave of movement through the quad. Mack's arms tighten around me and I tip my head, nestling further into the kiss.

I don't know what's going to happen from here.

I have no idea how long Mack's staying or even what the rest of this day holds...let alone our future. All I do know is that I'm right where I belong, and logic can stick it.

I'm in love with Mack Mahoney, and I'm not going to let a little thing like distance put a stop to that.

ONE LOOK CHANGED EVERYTHING

MACK

THE AIR IS COOL, but not cold. It's a refreshing tickle on my skin. I wrap my arms around Kaija, who's nestled in front of me. My legs are on either side of her. She's completely encased by me. I love that.

Her long fingers curl around my forearms as we gaze out at the ocean together. I can't believe the beauty of this place. Idaho is a land-locked state, and New Zealand is surrounded by water. It's insane. Kaija's house is a five-minute drive from about four different beaches. Right now, we're snuggled up on a picnic rug at Eastern Beach. Her school is up on the hill behind us, but we're facing the water. The islands in the distance are murky, black shapes, the moonlight not quite reaching them. It's sparkling off the water now, creating natural fairy lights that I can't stop watching.

We haven't said much since we arrived about an hour ago. Her parents have been nice enough to let me stay in their guest room downstairs. It's been an amazing two-week break—sightseeing, hanging out with her family, getting to know her friend Eloise. But I've got to get back. I timed the trip so I'd be here over Spring Break, and Mom let me take one extra week off school —not that she could have stopped me, but it was nice that she agreed. She even loaned me money for my ticket, and drove me to the airport.

Layla's picking me up, which is a good thing.

Something's up with that girl, and I need to find out what it is.

I asked Finn to watch out for her while I was away, but the last time we spoke he was really hedgy. Layla hasn't been much better. In fact, last time I tried to Skype, she refused and I made do with a long text conversation instead. She's always been crap at hiding things from me. Hopefully once we're together, she'll cave and tell me what the hell has been eating her. I'm also planning on grilling Finn. He's supposed to be stepping up and keeping her safe, but something in his communication has been amiss. I've got to get back and figure out what's going on.

But it means leaving Kaija. And I really am not looking forward to that part.

I nuzzle my lips into the crook of her neck, breathing her in, trying to memorize every smell, taste, and feel. Leaving her tomorrow is going to suck. We haven't really talked about our future, too busy making up for lost time. She skipped out of school a couple of times so we could spend the day together. She's been the world's sexiest tour guide, I can tell you that.

I'm totally in love with Auckland. It's the coolest city, surrounded by blue water, boats, and fitness freaks. I've never seen so many joggers and cyclists. New Zealand seems to thrive on healthy living. I could do well here.

I rest my chin on Kaija's shoulder and sigh.

"I don't want you to go either," she murmurs, gripping my arm as if it might make me stay.

"I know, but I gotta graduate."

"And check on your sister." She turns to look at me.

I force a smile that she sees straight through.

"I know you care about her a lot and I love that, but..." She purses her lips, her gaze skittering down to the ground before popping back up to mine. "She's not your responsibility."

My face bunches with an *I know* kind of frown. Kaija's

totally right. I'm not her father. I just feel so bad leaving her behind. When I was set to attend Boise State, I would have only been a three-hour drive away. That's peanuts—a day trip.

If I follow my heart, we're talking miles....like seven thousand of them.

"She's going to be okay." Kaija's fingers brush my light stubble before dipping into the dimple on my chin. She follows up the move with a kiss that makes me forget about time and space. I glide my hands up her back, spinning her around properly so she can sit in my lap. Her knees hug my butt, her body pressing against mine as I hold her close.

Her long hair falls forward, creating a curtain around us. I brush my tongue against hers, lost in the power she has over me. There's only one way I'm going to be able to leave tomorrow...and that's if I have the promise of coming back.

Pulling out of the kiss, I cup Kaija's face and look into those eyes that own me. "What if I apply to Auckland University? I read they do mid-year intakes, or I could find some kind of job to see me through the rest of this year, and then start with you in February."

Her smile is wide, her eyes sparkling as she whispers, "I'd like that."

"Yeah?"

"You know I would." She lightly slaps my shoulder with a laugh. "You sure you're willing to be that far from home?"

"I can't be that far from you, so…yeah, I'm sure."

Brushing her teeth over her bottom lip, she gives me another dynamic smile before shaking her head. "You know, when I fled this place looking for a new start, I never expected to find you. After what I did, it seems drastically unfair to be blessed this way."

I grin. "You're an unexpected surprise, as well. My life was set and you've turned it on its head." I brush my lips against hers and whisper, "Thank you."

She smiles down at me, running her thumbs beneath my eyes. "These eyes. You have no idea how powerful they are. Maybe that's why I tried to resist you so much in the beginning."

"I thought you were just overwhelmed by my charm and didn't know how to handle it."

She tips her head back, letting out that deep, belly laugh of hers. Damn, I love that sound. I press my lips to her exposed neck while she giggles, then teases me. "You still think you're such hot shit, don't you, mate?"

"Nah, you've blown that theory right out of the water." I grin. "Now, I'm just a guy who fell in love with a girl after only one look."

"You fell in lust with a girl after only one look. You fell in love trying to win me over."

"No." I shake my head and make sure she's looking at me. "One look changed everything for me. For us. Turns out love at first sight is actually a real thing."

"Well, aren't we the lucky ones."

"I'm never gonna forget it."

Her emerald eyes begin to sparkle and I wind my arms around her again. Her mouth claims mine and I remind myself to hang onto everything about this moment. This girl is mine. I am hers. And although we're saying goodbye tomorrow, we're going to be together forever.

Thank you so much for reading The Red Zone. I hope you enjoyed it. It was an absolute pleasure to write. If you'd like to show me some support, I'd love for you to leave a review… This is a great way to validate the book and let other people know what you thought of Mack & Kaija.

Would you like to find out who exposed Kaija's secret to Nelson High? And what's up with Tori's exciting news? More will be revealed in the last two Big Play Novels.

Keep reading to find out whose story is next!

THE HANDOFF

She's the last person he has time for, but Finn's never been able to turn his back on someone in trouble. Can the kind-hearted offensive lineman be won over by Nelson High's party girl?

It's nearly spring break. Mack is leaving for New Zealand to win back his girl, and he asks Finn (Tank) to do him a favor—keep an eye on his little sister, Layla. Finn has his reservations about the party girl, but he isn't about to let one of his best friends down, so he agrees. Unfortunately for him, he has no idea what he's getting into…or the effect this dynamic beauty will have on him.

Layla likes to party. It's the only sure-fire medicine for helping her forget the fact that her father's dead and a new guy has taken his place. But when she's drunk, Layla has a big mouth…and the wrong friends. Unable to remember what she's been up to at her various parties, Layla falls into a nasty trap.

Thanks to some compromising photographs, she is now under the thumb of the person she hates most in this world—her stepbrother, Derek. With Mack gone, she's forced to turn to someone who's always kept his distance, a good guy who has never had time for her partying ways. Letting Finn in on her dark and dirty secrets is something she never planned to do, but his tender strength and quiet protection draws it out of her, creating a bond between them that neither saw coming…and a whirlwind of problems that they'll only survive if they stick together.

Fans of redemptive love, nail-biting tension and heart-melting kisses will love *The Handoff*.

This compelling YA sports romance is available on Amazon

NOTE FROM THE AUTHOR

I actually came up with this story line a few years ago. When I started creating the Nelson High world, I figured it'd make a really good fit. I changed and adapted the original concept, of course, but the main premise is still the same. I really wanted to write a story from a bully's point of view. I wanted to create a redeemable character, someone who could learn from her mistakes and become a better person. Writing Kaija was an absolute pleasure. I love how she eventually faces up to her demons and owns her mistakes.

I also love Mack's journey. It's so easy to fall in line with everyone else's expectations. Finding the courage to break the mold can be really hard, and I love how Kaija exposes Mack's independent streak and allows him to chase after the things he really wants.

I know some people scoff at love at first sight or stories involving insta-love, but I do think it exists. Some people are lucky enough to meet their soulmate and know it after one look. It's been a total thrill being able to portray a love story like this.

If you're looking for me in the book, you'll find me in Eloise. I was the Kiwi Girl who lived in remote parts of the world and returned to Macleans College, the clueless, frightened kid with the weird accent. Thankfully for me, I wasn't bullied to the same degree and I never reacted the way Eloise did, but I understood her pain. High school can be a mighty ocean, and it can get pretty lonely there sometimes. I'm so grateful to my supportive parents who helped me find my courage and who wouldn't let me hide away like I so desperately wanted to.

As always, this book is a group effort. I want to thank Rae, Cassie & Beth for being so instrumental in making Mack and Kaija's story what it should be. Thanks again to my awesome brother for the flea flicker play suggestion, and to my husband for making sure I got the rugby and rugby league stuff right! I grew up in a very sporty family and I've married a sports nut, as well, so it's great to be surrounded by so much knowledge.

Thank you to my amazing proofreaders and my advanced reader team. Your opinions, reviews, corrections, and all-out love for these characters inspire and motivate me. You guys are the best.

To everyone who has read this book, thank you for your time. I really hope you enjoyed it. I can't wait to share the rest of this senior year with you!

And finally, I'd like to give a special mention to God. Every story is a gift from Him, and I want to thank Him for helping me craft *The Red Zone*.

xx
Jordan

Made in the USA
Columbia, SC
12 January 2020